THIS WILL NEVER HAPPEN...

Matthew Nath

ISBN 978-1-63903-602-8 (paperback)
ISBN 978-1-63903-603-5 (digital)

Christian Faith Publishing, Inc.
832 Park Avenue
Meadville, PA 16335
www.christianfaithpublishing.com

Printed in the United States of America

CHAPTER 1

The bell rang out, waking Rhys to a new day. He woke quickly and sat up, swinging his legs off the bed before he fell back asleep. One time doing that was trouble enough. He cringed as he felt the dirt fill the space between his toes. He really wished he could get used to it, but the gritty feeling still made him sick. He stood from his mattress on the floor and reached out for his tattered clothing, sighing at the feeling of the thin fabric between his fingers. Grace did what she could to keep it together, but there were still rips along the body and the back. *At least she tries*, he thought to himself, *and it's a lot more than I could do myself.* He pulled his shirt over his head and smiled down at the bundled form of his still sleeping wife on the mattress on the floor.

She was lying on her side in bed, facing him, with a pillow pulled up against her chest. Rhys smiled at her, knowing she would be up soon but enjoying the contented look she was able to get from their still warm bed. He felt his heart warm and said a quick prayer thanking God for his beautiful wife. He turned and walked through the curtain blocking off their bedroom.

Rhys stepped into a dark narrow hallway. His children's room was on his right, and a small bathroom was across the hall. The houses in the Color district were built back-to-back in a long row of narrow shacks to fit as many as possible. Each house had the same layout and was divided into four sections, living room in front-right followed by kitchen, bathroom and closets, and bedrooms in the front-left. Large, open windows filled the front of the house so the Colors could be monitored at all times for the protection of the Whites.

When Rhys finished his morning routine, he stepped into his children's room. "Time to get up," he said gently. Thomas sat up immediately and stared at him through confused eyes. He rubbed his eyes as he stood from his mattress and started to get dressed. His daughter hadn't moved yet.

"Lillian," Rhys called quietly, "you need to get up. You can't be late for school." Lily grunted in response. "Come on," Rhys coaxed, "its Thomas's first day. You want to be able to show him around, right?" Rhys smiled at Thomas's eager face. Lily grunted again and then threw the covers off her body. Rhys left them to get dressed and went to start breakfast.

He stoked the fire in the living room before adding another log to the large stone fireplace. The fire roared back to life, flames licking the bottom of a pot hanging above. Rhys opened the lid of the kettle and stirred whatever they were served for food inside. Rhys tried to break up the gelatinous mass, a faint memory filling his mind of growing up and having oatmeal cooked for too long in the microwave. He didn't think oatmeal was usually quite as thick as the stuff he was stirring now though. He added some water from the last of their bottles, and watched the gruel finally break apart. Rhys sighed before scooping four bowls out, emptying the pot completely.

He pulled the pot off the fire and set it in the window's edge to cool, smiling as a small black cat jumped up. The past three weeks, the same cat had been coming to Rhys's window. He had named it Bear, but he kept that to himself. Rhys ran a hand over the cat's head as it stuck its nose into the still warm pot. Rhys scooped a small amount of his breakfast onto the window ledge and watched as the cat started eating.

"Is he here?" an eager voice called out from the hall. Rhys was setting out the bowls around the kitchen table, enjoying his son's fascination with anything living when Thomas came bolting out of his room, half dressed. Rhys stopped to watch his son slowly make his way toward the window.

"Hey Kissy," Thomas said cooingly. The cat glared back with a blank stare.

"I don't think he likes that name," Rhys laughed.

"Well what do you call him?" Thomas asked, over his shoulder, still sneaking slowly toward the window. Lily entered the kitchen, sleepily rubbing at her eyes. She sat down at the table and started eating her breakfast, eyes only half open.

"Good morning, sunshine" Rhys said to Lily.

"That's a dumb name," Thomas joked to his dad.

"Har har," Rhys replied, sarcastically. "And I call him Bear." As soon as Rhys said *Bear*, the cat jumped into the house. Thomas grabbed at him, but Bear dodged his arms and dashed to Rhys's legs. "Careful," Rhys said imploringly to Thomas. "He's a stray, he might bite."

Thomas was determined. He calmed himself and crept toward the cat, repeating, "Bear," in various different sing song voices. The cat eventually walked over to Thomas and allowed itself to be pet. After a few moments, the cat dashed across the floor and out the window. Rhys sighed as he thought for the thousandth time how nice it would be to put a curtain over that window.

"Alright," Rhys said, shaking himself back. He glanced out the window at the armed Gray, standing in the center of the path outside their shack. The cat had drawn the guard's attention and he was watching Rhys through the window. Rhys stopped what he was doing, and bowed his head to the Gray, whispering a quick, silent prayer to God while he held the pose. After a few seconds he looked up, relieved to see that the guard had moved on. He quickly moved back into the kitchen and into the privacy afforded by a wall that blocked about half the room from view. It was the only semi-private room of their house, aside from the bathroom.

Rhys sat at the table and joined hands with his children. "Mom, are you coming?" Lily called out. They heard some shuffling as Grace hustled down the hall. She sat and grabbed the waiting hands of her children. Rhys led the family in a hushed, whispered prayer of Thanksgiving for the meal and for the day. Their prayer ended with entire family, very quietly, reciting the Lord's Prayer. When they were finished praying, they dropped their hands and started eating.

"You ready for today?" Rhys asked his wife from across the table.

Grace quickly swallowed before replying, "I think so. I'm gonna have to be, right?"

Rhys could read the anxiety in her voice, but knew she was trying to hide it so he didn't call attention to it. "You're gonna do great," he replied with a smile.

Grace met his eyes and smiled back. She continued, "It's just been so long. I know I pretty much grew up in the Garden but it's been years. What if things are totally different now?"

Rhys reached across the small table and put his hand over his wife's. "You'll do great, dear. You know what you're doing. And things never change around here, right?" He ended his sentence with a chuckle and was glad to see Grace's shoulders relax slightly as she smiled back.

"And what about you, Thomas? Are you excited for your first day at school?" Rhys asked his son.

"Yep!" Thomas replied through a mouth full of food.

"Ugh," Lily said, "don't talk with your mouth full like that. You're going to spray me with something. Can't you just be a human?" Thomas opened his mouth wide, showing off his food to his sister. "Dad!" Lily said.

"Thomas, I know you like being gross but can you try to be civil for the rest of us?"

Thomas swallowed and smiled at his dad. "Yes. And yes, I am excited for school. What do you think I'm going to learn?"

"You'll learn your place, mostly," Rhys replied with a sigh. Thomas deflated a little bit, watching his dad. "We've told you, bud, you aren't there to learn. You're there to be shown how to behave, how to show respect, and how to not get into trouble."

"I know," Thomas said, talking quickly again now. "I know I sit in the back and keep silent. Don't worry, I know what to do and I promise I won't get in trouble. But I'm excited to see what they can teach me. I want to read better and I want to learn to use numbers better. I think I can learn some of that stuff there, right?"

"Maybe," Rhys replied. It warmed his heart to see his son's excitement about learning, but he needed to temper his expectations. "The only classes they let you sit in on are the social studies classes though. They don't want you to learn too much. Yes, while you're there you might be able to see some different lessons. You might catch a part of a math class, or science class. But don't be too curious. Don't stand out right now. Try not to bring attention to yourself."

"I know, dad," Thomas replied seriously. "I know. And I'll be careful."

"And I'll be there to keep an eye on the gross-o," Lily interjected with a smile. "I can show him the ropes and make sure he's keeping his nose out of things and his head down."

Rhys smiled at Lily and then looked admiringly at his wife. "How did those monsters we used to have turn into such good kids?" She smiled and shook her head in response.

"I don't know, but we must have done something right," she said.

"Not you guys," Lily said after a moment. She continued quietly, almost under her breath, "it was God. God *and* you guys." A clever smile lit her face as she continued, "and I'm still the monster you knew, God just helps me keep it under control."

"I gotta finish getting ready," Grace said. She started bringing her plate to the sink, but Rhys stood and grabbed it from her hands.

"You don't want to be late," he said with a smile, giving her a gentle kiss. "I'll clean up, you go get ready." Grace kissed him back, and smiled appreciatively as she turned and left the kitchen.

"You guys are the gross ones," Thomas chimed in. He brought is plate to the sink and went to get his shoes on. Lily followed close after while Rhys quickly scraped out their bowls, combining what was left into one. Then he brought that bowl and set it on the window ledge. Almost immediately, Bear jumped up and started eating. Rhys smiled and started petting behind the cat's ears. He looked up and met eyes with the same Gray. Rhys quickly bowed his head.

Rhys kept his gaze down, but watched the man's feet as he walked closer to the window. He stopped just short of the building and Rhys couldn't take his eyes off the large, black gun the man had strapped around his neck.

"He yours?" the man asked.

7

Rhys took a breath and then replied, "No, sir. Just a stray. He comes here to eat but that's it." Rhys was careful to keep his gaze down while he talked. His instincts seemed to be pushing at him to meet the man's eyes.

"Ah," the man grunted in response. A silence filled the air that was eventually broken by the Gray with, "Well, better get ready. You'll be expected at work soon."

"Yes, sir," Rhys replied.

"For All Are One," the Gray said.

"And One Serves All," Rhys replied.

Rhys watched as the Gray turned and walked slowly back to the center of the path. Once he was sure the man wasn't going to come back, Rhys stood and went back to the kitchen. He waited there for his family to join him, his heart still pounding in his chest. His family needed to see him be brave so he pulled his shoulders back and smiled as they returned to the room.

They gathered behind the wall in the kitchen when they were all ready. Rhys leaned over, glancing out the window. Seeing that the coast was clear, he put his arm around his wife's shoulders. He pulled her and the children into a tight hug and held it for their prayer.

Rhys began, speaking very quietly, "May the Lord bless us and keep us; may He make His face shine upon us and be gracious to us; and may He grant us peace through our day. Amen."

"Amen," the rest of the family replied quietly.

They broke up but Rhys held Grace a moment longer. He gave her a short kiss while the kids were leaving the room, then followed them out. They closed the door behind them, and Rhys found himself wishing for the thousandth time that he could secure the door somehow. He waved to his children who walked toward the city, and then turned and walked the other way. On the path around him were dozens of other men, all dressed in dirty, tattered, colorful clothing. They all walked in the same manner, with a slow shuffle and their heads bowed. No one wanted to draw attention to himself. Rhys joined the group and started his day.

CHAPTER 2

⁓

G race slowed for a moment, taking a deep breath as she walked past the orchids. The smell reminded her of her youth. She jumped as the woman walking behind her shoved her shoulder forward. Grace looked back apologetically only to be met with an angry glare. Grace bowed her head and stepped forward in line, moving slowly toward the steel door and the Gray guards.

When it was her turn, she held out her left forearm, displaying her tattoos. These marked which work group she was a part of. For the past fifteen years she had been assigned to the child care center. But, since Thomas was entering his tenth year, she was finally able to return to the Gardens where she had received her training. The guard absently glanced at her arm and then nodded, looking toward the woman in line behind her. Grace stepped off the dirt path and through the door.

The scent of life filled her nostrils as she felt herself gliding across the smooth, clean metal floor. She looked slowly around the room, taking it all in. The large, bright windows, the posters covering nearly every open wall surface. Even the strangely colored brown, metal boxes hanging from the ceiling made her smile. She hadn't realized until this moment how much she had missed the Garden. She tried to keep her emotions in check as she followed the slow moving line.

When she was to the front of the line, a Gray motioned her forward. He pointed to a clean, metal table and said, "You, get to work."

Grace bowed her head and pulled her dress out in a curtsey. The Gray grunted in response before moving on, taking the rest of the women with him. Grace sighed and turned to her table. She tried to remember her training, but it wasn't complicated. Her work was very simple and she was only given the materials she would need at that time. It looked like her first task would be watering, as there were several watering cans in front of her, as well as a bag of fertilizer.

Grace knew her task was to fill the cans with fertilizer, then with water from the spout. She was allowed to carry only one can at a time. The walk there and back was patrolled by a Gray and talking to other Colors was prohibited while working. Honestly though, that was not a problem for Grace. She had a hard time trusting the other Colors. They always seemed to be on the lookout for ways to get you in trouble.

The table next to her was about six feet away and filled with different supplies. Each woman was assigned a different task. When all the women were at their assigned tables, a soft gong rang out. Grace remembered it to mean she was to begin her work. She measured and scooped out the fertilizer from the bag, weighing it in her hand and then dumping it into the watering can.

When all of her buckets were filled, she turned to the center, indicating she was ready to be escorted to the spout. A Gray standing nearby nodded to her and motioned for her to start walking. Grace walked quickly, trying not to notice the large signs hanging on the wall. "SEE SOMETHING, SAY SOMETHING" and "THE WHITES PROVIDE ALL, WE PROVIDE HONOR TO THE WHITES." Grace set her bucket on the ground under the spout and started pumping the handle to get the water flowing.

When her bucket was full, she picked it up and turned to start her walk back to the table. As she turned, she felt the side of her bucket bump lightly into something. In horror, she watched as a small amount of water splashed out of the bucket and onto the pure, untainted robes of a White. Her eyes moved up the robes before briefly meeting his. He gave her a vicious smile for a brief moment, then his face contorted to something evil and angry.

"You dare!" he screamed. The room fell silent as all Colors dropped to their knees, pressing their faces to the ground in supplication. The Grays dropped to one knee and placed a hand on their forehead. Grace realized too late that she was the only one still standing. It had taken her mind some time to catch up to the scene and in those few seconds, everyone else around her had already bowed. She dropped to her knees, attempting to set down the bucket at the same time. In her haste, the bucket tipped over. She was unable to do anything to stop it, and could only watch as the water rushed over the white robes. She kept her head bowed, trying to hold back tears.

The entire room fell deathly quiet. The Colors waited in fear and the Grays were awaiting orders. Grace could only see the White's robes as he stood in silence above her. Grace kept her head down and perfectly still, not sure what to do. She had never seen this happen before and didn't know what to expect.

Chills ran down her spine as the metal tip of a cane slide along her neck and onto her cheek. The cane rested on her chin and pulled up slightly. Grace followed the cane up, lifting first her head, then her entire body until she stood facing the White.

"You see what you've done?" the White said in a quiet voice. Grace, not sure if he was expecting an answer or not, only met his eyes and nodded silently. The man smiled that vicious smile again while meeting her eyes. Grace was curious at the slightly yellow hue to the man's eyes. She also noticed a deep purple color under each eye. Grace had never seen a White so closely before.

"What to do, what to do?" the man said, more to himself than anyone else. "The knife? No that would be a waste. A Gray in the interrogation room?" He gave himself a little shrug and began surveying the Grays around the room. His face dropped slightly as he finished his scan. Grace felt her stomach knot up at the thought of any of those Grays taking her outside.

"This is the drab they have watching you? Ugh. None here are deserving of any gifts from me. Guess that means it's your lucky day," he said meeting her eyes again. Grace closed her eyes and said a quick, silent prayer of thanks to God for His protection. She opened her eyes and the White was staring at her with a curious look in his eye.

"What was that?" he asked. It sounded like an innocent question, but Grace detected a hint of excitement behind his voice.

"What was what, your holiness?" Grace stuttered in reply.

"That," he asked, pressing the metal tip of the cane harder into her chin. "You closed your eyes."

Grace shook her head. She didn't know how but he seemed to know that she had prayed. "I'm sorry sir, it was nothing. I was only-"

"Silence," the White said, cutting her off. He didn't seem to have heard anything she said. He looked away from her for a moment, surveying the room again. He stood slightly taller then took one final check around the room. Satisfied with whatever he was looking for, he began speaking loudly enough for the entire room to hear.

"You should be killed for this transgression. But, I will show you mercy and grace. I understand you Colors are weak and clumsy people. After what your ancestors did to mine, I believe your 'accident' here was done intentionally, in an attempt to sully my purity. But, I will not sink to your level. As we all know, the Whites are incapable of violence but I will instruct my Grays guarding you today to show no violence either. As punishment instead, you will report to the Tower this afternoon and wash my robes personally by hand. This act of service will offer a path for penance and for you to show you hold a properly repentant attitude."

With that, he turned and began strolling out of the building. Grace watched the man's oversized figure shamble toward the door in shock; unsure what had just happened. She thought about her new task and realized she had no idea how to complete it. Grace panicked at seeing the door about to close.

"But, sir," she shouted, "how will I find you in the Tower?"

The White froze in place, not acknowledging her statement for a moment. "You deem yourself worthy of addressing me? And, worse, to assume my gender?! As all present should know, the proper pronoun should be zir!" The silent tension, almost cleared a moment ago, redoubled in the room. All stood silent, watching the White. Grace felt a wave of nausea starting as she realized what she'd done. She held her breath, waiting for further response.

Finally, after what felt like an hour, the White spoke, not turning to face anyone. "You test my patience and my mercy. Obviously you are to ask a Gray for guidance." With that, he strode out the door and into the bright daylight air. Grace felt herself deflate, realizing she was still holding her breath. She dropped to the ground, praying to God for strength to keep from crying. She took a deep, unsteady breath and picked up her bucket.

Grace turned back to the wall, completing the task she started what felt like ages ago. When her bucket was filled, she began her walk back to her work desk. She made eye contact with the Gray escorting her.

"That was Connors. How are you not dead?" the Gray asked as they walked. It almost sounded to Grace like the young man was concerned for her. Grace's mind was racing over the conversation in her head. She felt like there was a lot more importance to what Connors had said, but she couldn't understand it all. She gave up and focused on watering the plants in front of her, trying hard not to spill again.

CHAPTER 3

Rhys held his hand up as he looked toward the sun, trying to gauge the time. The sun was brutally hot today and it had to be getting close to lunch, which was a nice break no matter how short it was. He was most looking forward to the water so he could cool himself off some. His motion had caught the attention of a Gray, who yelled at him to get back to work. Rhys offered a slight bow, placing his hands together in front of his face, before turning picking up a board and bringing it back to the wall.

He found a place with a small gap and covered it, nailing the wooden board in place. The haphazardness of the work drove him nuts, but he could only do what he was told. He could tell the wall was far weaker than it needed to be. Well, except for a raised portion called the wall walk, which had been built years ago and rarely needed fixing. The Grays were able to patrol around the entire Complex from that walk. Rhys had been assigned wall duty today, which meant patching together the lower wall with a random assortment of boards. He worked hard and did his best to not to show too much annoyance at his fellow Color's shoddy work.

But then, what would they have the Colors do if not fixing the wall? *Fixing our homes,* Rhys thought to himself. He was glad not to be out scavenging at least. The boards Rhys was using were being gathered by other Colors from the hundreds of abandoned houses that surrounded the Complex. Those houses were sometimes occupied by the rebels who were ready to kill anyone who entered.

The Colors were also guarded more closely by the Gray's while they scavenged, putting them in a more vulnerable position. Rhys had found himself on the bad end of a Gray's abuse too many times to count. Luckily the abuse was monitored, if casually, by the White overseeing this part of the wall. If the abuse caused harm to any Color's ability to scavenge, the Gray would lose his robes and be sent out to scavenge as a Color instead. So the beatings were careful and controlled. But still an ever present threat. Rhys did his best to keep his head down and keep out of trouble.

Lunch came and went without incident. Rhys was assigned a new location near some woods for the afternoon. When he realized he would be in the shade of the trees for the rest of the day, Rhys offered a silent prayer of Thanksgiving to God. As he worked, he tried to hide the joy he felt after having prayed. He realized that he hadn't hidden it very well when another Color working nearby grunted to get Rhys's attention.

Rhys met the man's confused gaze and could only smile in response. The man looked over his shoulder, checking the distance to the nearest Gray. When he was sure he could talk without being heard, the man said quietly, "Why are you smiling, man?"

Rhys prayed to God for protection and trusted the feeling of peace that came over him. "Just feeling blessed to be in the shade, I guess," Rhys replied with a shrug. He looked over his shoulder to ensure the Grays weren't nearby, then folded his hands in front of his face pressing his fingers to his lips and his thumbs to his chin. He offered a silent but exaggerated prayer to God that he would open this man's heart so he may see the truth. Rhys turned back to work, and a moment later the man did too. Rhys noticed a thoughtful look on the man's face. Over the next few hours, Rhys saw the man start to say something, but stop himself. Rhys smiled and continued working, thinking how great it would be if they could just talk.

Rhys jumped as he heard a noise in the trees behind him. The hairs on the back of his neck stood up as he turned and watched the trees carefully. In front of him was a steep slope down, followed by about ten feet of grass before the edge of the forest. He felt like he was being watched but couldn't see anything moving. Then, all of a sudden, a large doe jumped out of the trees and started grazing on the grass.

Rhys knew what he was supposed to do, raise his arm and point out the animal so the snipers guarding the wall knew where to shoot. The only problem is that as often as not, they shot at the Colors too. Rhys looked around to his fellow workers, knowing if it wasn't him it would be one of them. He sighed, and raised his arm, looking to the sky at the same time and praying as hard as he could to God for protection.

A full minute passed. Rhys stood still, keeping one arm in the air and another arm pointing toward the doe. He realized the doe was staring at him and Rhys could do nothing but stare back. The silence along the wall indicated that those around him had taken notice. They were waiting for the-

BANG! The sound reverberated through the air, causing Rhys to jump. He hated these first few seconds after the shot, when you never knew for sure if you've been hit or not. Rhys fell after he jumped and found himself rolling down the steep hill, landing a few feet away from the doe. He did a mental assessment of himself and realized that he was OK.

He caught his breath then started to stand. BANG! A second shot rang out and Rhys felt the bullet as it ripped through the air next to him. He panicked and dropped to the ground, covering his head. Rhys didn't know if he should stand or stay down. After a few seconds, he noticed that the deer was still alive. Rhys could hear her breathing and bleating in pain.

"Color!" the voice of a Gray rang out. "Get back to your station and back to work."

Rhys sighed, praying to God once more that the Gray wouldn't shoot him. He stood and said, "I beg of you sir, I dropped my hammer, please may I search for it?" The Gray stood above him on the hill and glared down. Rhys kept his head bowed as he waited for a response.

"Well, you ain't gonna be much good without it now will ya?" the Gray responded. Rhys bowed deeper and then turned, kicking his hammer closer to the deer. Rhys made a show of kicking grass aside to try to find it as he moved closer to the deer. He had seen this before and knew how poorly the Gray's treated these animals. Once it was clear the deer was hit and couldn't get away, they left it there to suffer and die.

Rhys remembered when he was very young, maybe ten years old, hunting with his dad. His dad taught him how long and painful a death like that can be for an animal. It can take hours, even days sometimes. All the while, the poor animal is lying in fear and pain. Wanting to survive and wanting to move, but unable to. Rhys couldn't let this poor deer go through that. Not if there was something he could do to help.

He got close enough to the deer that he could take care of it. He bent down to grab his hammer and quickly slammed the clawed end into the skull of the doe. Almost immediately, the breathing and bleating stopped. Rhys watched it for a moment, then bowed his head and covered the doe's eyes with his hand. He spoke a short, quiet prayer to God, "Thank you Lord for the strength and opportunity to remove suffering from this poor animal. Amen."

Rhys stood, holding his hammer up. He started back toward the wall, the Gray watching him carefully. Rhys thought he heard something move behind him as he started away from the doe, and was worried that he hadn't finished it. Rhys looked at the doe and saw that it was clearly dead. He glanced into the forest one more time before climbing the hill to finish his shift.

CHAPTER 4

Thomas and Lily walked side by side down the narrow, dirty alley. Thomas was kicking a rock along the way and humming a tune under his breath. Lily was holding up a small, clean piece of metal and looking at her reflection. She played with her hair, trying to get it just right, while keeping an eye on Thomas. They rounded a corner and Lily stopped cold.

Ahead of them was a chain link fence, with a bright, clean road just on the other side. Lily saw a White walking slowly down the road, surrounded by several Grays on their knees. Lily froze for a second, not sure what to do. Usually when you first saw a White, custom was to bow and hold your head against the ground until the White had passed or an order was given. But, Lily was fairly certain the Whites wouldn't be looking into the alley at them. Just to be safe, she grabbed Thomas's overlarge shirt and pulled him to his knees.

They sat a moment in silence, before Thomas whispered, "Uh, Lily, what are we doing?"

"Shh," Lily replied, trying to listen for any sign of the White having passed. When she heard the normal bustle of walking, whispering people, she breathed a sigh of relief. If there was trouble, the street would either be in an eerie silence, or it would be loud as the Grays moved into action. She slowly lifted her eyes, surveying the street ahead of them. Noticing nothing out of the ordinary, Lily took her hand off Thomas's shoulder and stood up.

"That was weird," he replied, dusting off his already dirty clothes.

"No, that's what you do. You ever see a White, you do what we just did," Lily replied. "You're not with the Colors anymore. The Whites never come to the Color district, so you haven't had to worry about it, but you might see them now. And you do not want their attention on you." She shook her head, relieved at having dodged a bullet, maybe literally. She held the piece of metal in front of her again and continued trying to straighten her hair.

Thomas looked thoughtful for a minute then started walking again. After a few moments of silence, he motioned to her hair and asked, "Why do you even try? You're never happy with it."

Lily shouldn't have been surprised but was worried that he wasn't taking the Whites seriously enough. She did the only thing she could and prayed to God that He watch over Thomas and protect him. Then she replied, motioning to his arms as he brushed dirt off his shirt, "Why do you try that? Those clothes are at least third level hand-me-downs. Mom found that shirt on the side of the road. Pretty sure you're not gonna get it clean."

"It's my first day," Thomas said, a little hurt. "I just wanna look good." Thomas continued wiping the dirt away. Lily sighed and helped get her brother's back. He smiled at her over his shoulder as they neared the fence. A large, intimidating looking Gray stood on the other side, watching them over his shoulder but facing toward the street. Lily and Thomas nodded respect to the Gray waiting for him to dismiss them. He grunted and turned his back to them, facing the open street and eyes turned toward the departing White.

Lily grabbed the knob of a worn wooden door loosely fit over a hole in the brick wall. She grunted slightly as she lifted up on the knob and pulled the door open, revealing a dark, narrow hallway.

"This is how we have to get in?" Thomas asked.

"I told you, Thomas, they don't let us in the front." Lily replied. "They don't want us to dirty a White. We use this door instead."

"But there's no candles, and I can see spider webs there," Thomas said. Lily could hear a hint of genuine fear in his voice.

"It's fine bud," Lily tried to use a gentle voice, hoping it would calm her brother. She put a hand on his shoulder and continued. "It'll be fine. I promise. You'll get used to it. We walk this same hall every day for the next few years. Nothing's gonna get you. You'll be fine."

Thomas took a steadying breath before stepping into the schoolhouse. Lily followed down the narrow hall and around the outside of the building. They walked the length of the building, unfinished, rotted wooden walls on one side, and cracking brick on the other. Small holes knocked into the brick let in just enough light to see where they were going. Thomas let out a small squeal as a rat darted across the hall in front of him, hiding in a hole in the brick.

Eventually the hall turned left. They continued for a few feet until coming to another narrow wooden door. Lily stopped for a moment and gestured to the door. "This is you," she said.

Thomas visibly gulped and then stepped into the room. Lily smiled, said another quick prayer, and then made her way to her classroom, following the hall back toward the entrance.

* * *

Thomas entered into another world. He left the dark, musty hallway and entered a clean, well lit classroom. Two rows of brightly lit circles ran along the ceiling that Thomas had never seen before. Each circle looked like a tiny sun. His parents had tried to prepare him about the lights, but it hadn't helped. He felt his mouth hanging open at their beauty. He smiled and dropped his gaze down.

The walls on either side of him were adorned with the usual posters: FOR ALL ARE ONE AND ONE SERVES ALL. REPORT ANY ODD BEHAVIOR TO YOUR GRAYS. ALL HONOR TO THE WHITES, ALL MERCY FROM THE WHITES. Thomas took in the large windows on either side of an ornate wooden door at the front of the room. On the other side of the windows was the street he had just seen through the metal of the fence.

He stood facing two rows of desks. The front few were large, elaborate desks. Each desk held a small, black box that seemed to have lights of their own that Thomas had never seen before. Behind these were a few more light wooden desks with just paper and a pencil. Thomas turned his eyes along the back wall and saw a row of metal chairs. Two of the chairs were filled with other Color students.

Thomas smiled at them as he walked to an empty metal chair. The girl offered a weak smile in response but the boy just stared straight ahead, not acknowledging Thomas at all. Thomas took his seat and waited. Children started filing into the room, Grays from the front door and other Color students from the back door Thomas had used. Within ten minutes, the chairs were filled except those in the front.

A whistle rang out along the street and all of the Grays immediately stood at attention. The Color students looked at each other. No one seemed sure what to do. Eventually, they all stood as well, though furtive glances continued to be exchanged between the kids. The room waited in silence, watching the front doors.

A loud noise filled the empty air from the back of the room as the door slammed open. A frantic looking young boy jumped into the room, pushed the door shut behind himself, and then stood with the other Color students, trying to catch his breath. A few seconds later, the front door opened and a White teacher and three young White students entered the room. The Whites took their seats, ignoring the rest of the room. Once the Whites were seated, the Grays offered some type of salute and said in unison: "For All Are One." Then they took their seats. The Color students in the back kept their heads down, still unsure what to do. After a few seconds, they took their seats, one by one at first and then in a rush. None of the children wanted to be first or last at anything.

"Welcome, class," the teacher said loudly, looking only to the White students in the front row, but speaking in a tone to indicate that the entire room should listen. "My name is Mrs. Voss. In this class we will spend the next three years teaching you some of the most important topics including gender studies, social sciences, sexual education, and history. These classes are taught away from the Complex so that all children may be present, Whites, Grays, and Colors. No matter our role, these lessons will be essential to your correct behavior in society. Colors are here to listen only, and will not speak unless spoken to."

While Mrs. Voss was speaking, Thomas noticed the young boy who came in last. He tried to find a metal chair when they all sat down, but none were available. He looked around panicked, unsure of what to do. Thomas wanted to help him, but had no ideas either. For one insane moment, he thought about suggesting the boy use one of the empty White chairs.

As the seconds passed, the boy's face became more and more frantic. He eventually leaned up against the wall, half standing and half sitting. He looked like he was pretending to have a chair. Mrs. Voss looked up at the end of her speech and noticed the boy for the first time.

"And just what do you think you're doing?" she asked. Thomas could feel the hatred and anger in her voice. The boy stared back at her, mouth moving but no noise coming out, face stuck with a shocked expression.

"Think you're too good to sit?" Mrs. Voss continued. Her voice got louder and more excited as she kept talking. "See class? After generations, the Colors have still learned nothing. After all these years. After everything the Whites were put through before the Divide. You'd think he would have been taught how to act. That his fellow Colors would have had the decency to teach him about the shame he should feel."

Mrs. Voss stepped out from behind her podium and addressed the White students directly. "Do you know why he stands?" she asked. "He stands because he still thinks he should be above you. He thinks he is better. He stands because, were he to hit you, he'd need to be standing. His ancestors stood over your ancestors and he does the same. He stands to demonstrate his size and power over you, to show you he should be the one in charge."

The room stared in silence, looking back at the boy. The boy remained perfectly still as all eyes were on him. Thomas could see that his eyes were filled with tears. Mrs. Voss took a deep breath and continued, "He has already failed us. Already shown us his true nature. The true nature of all Colors without the mercy and guidance of the Whites. What is your name boy?"

The boy's mouth twitched but nothing came out. He coughed and cleared his throat, then whispered a name.

"You need to be much louder than that," Mrs. Voss said loudly.

"Isaiah," the boy replied, more loudly this time.

"Of course," Mrs. Voss replied, visibly upset. She grabbed on to the podium as if she had been physically hit. "Your caregivers must have no compassion. They care nothing for the suffering of my people, suffering that continues to this day because of hateful people like you. A disgusting name from that horrendous book. The book that led to the genocide of millions upon millions of Whites. At the hands of Colors like you."

She stood for a moment with her hand to her mouth, as if holding back tears. The room hung on her every word. She closed her eyes and said quietly, as if to herself but far too loud to not be heard, "Yes, I must punish him." She steadied herself, then looked up and said, "Young man, come to the front."

Isaiah stood rooted to the spot, unable to make himself move. When he didn't move fast enough, Mrs. Voss snapped her fingers and said, "Help him up here." Immediately three Grays leapt from their seats and grabbed Isaiah by the arms. They drug him to the front of the room. "I hate to have this done young man, but you need to be taught a lesson. As I am a White, I am obviously not capable of harming you, but I'm sure I can find some volunteers to assist me."

At this, every Gray jumped out of their seats and stood at attention. Thomas jumped up in fright at the speed of their response. Mrs. Voss smiled at the room and selected two seemingly random Gray students. They reported to the front. Mrs. Voss was humming happily to herself as she reached behind the door and pulled out a thin wooden rod about three feet long. She stood in front of Isaiah who was on his knees at the front of the classroom.

"Now class," Mrs. Voss said, "I do not want to have to do this, but this young man has left me no choice. His obstinence, his refusal to listen, his refusal to show the proper attitude toward those he's wronged, and his filthy name show me that he is in need of this lesson. This is a crisis. I think we are all in need of this lesson. I know this will be a reminder to many of you, but for those in the back, pay attention. I will tell you what will become of this child if his selfish ways are not stopped now.

"I hope we have stopped it in time, but this boy may be evil enough to become a hate filled Christian. Especially with a name like that. Years ago, before the Divide, the Christians allowed themselves to be filled with hate. If not stopped, his base impulses will grow until he loses control. Then, history will repeat itself as he slaughters as many Grays and Whites as he can. He will kill because he hates the color of our skin. Hates our choice in bedmates. Hates our gender expression. For thousands of years his ancestors found thousands of reasons to hate. And that hatred drove them insane. If not stopped early, all Colors are compelled to hatred. I say this now for all of you. Learn…your…place." She stared intently at each student in the back row before turning her attention back to Isaiah.

She handed the rod to the Grays who laid it across the floor. Isaiah maintained the pose of supplication, head on the ground and arms stretched forward toward the White. The Grays placed the rod over his hands. The White nodded and a Gray stood on one the end of the rod, while the other Gray lifted his side, positioning it over Isaiah's hands. When Thomas realized what they were going to do, he yelled out, "No!"

He put his hands over his mouth for a second, shocked at what he'd done. He mentally kicked himself but knew it was too late. He took a deep breath and forced himself to stand. He couldn't ignore his terror but also couldn't just watch. He had to do something. Had to try. Thomas blurted out, "I am so sorry goddess, but it wasn't his fault,"

A moment of silence followed, so Thomas continued on, piecing together a story as quickly as he could and praying he wouldn't be interrupted. "I stole his chair and forced him to stand. I came in late and saw he had a chair and I didn't want to get in trouble so I took his chair and I made him stand."

Mrs. Voss glared at Thomas from the front of the room for a moment. "Fine," she replied, "you get up here then."

Thomas felt his stomach drop as he realized what that meant. He hesitated for a second, but quickly realized there was no getting out of it. He steeled himself, preparing for the pain, took a deep breath, and then walked up toward the front. Isaiah started to stand when Mrs. Voss's voice cut in.

"Where do you think you're going?" she asked.

Isaiah couldn't reply. He just stopped moving, and put his head back on the ground. He tried to stifle it, but he let out a small sob as he put his hands back under the rod. Thomas dropped to his knees, extending his arms out so his hands were even with Isaiah's. He held his breath, anticipating the pain. He tented his fingers slightly, hoping that would relieve some of the pressure on Isaiah's hands.

The rod slapped down against the tops of his hands with more force than he would have thought possible. He didn't hear any cracks, but it felt like his fingers or knuckles were broken. His tented hands were struck hard against the ground. Thomas glanced up as the rod started rising again, noticing a shine of blood on the dirty wood.

Neither Thomas nor Isaiah had cried out with the first hit. Thomas said a silent prayer for strength to endure, took a deep breath, and closed his eyes. He wasn't able to keep silent for any of the remaining five blows.

CHAPTER 5

"Now that we have dealt with that unpleasantness, we can move forward with the lesson," Mrs. Voss said. Thomas rushed to take his seat as quickly and quietly as possible so as not to disrupt the lesson. As he moved, Mrs. Voss resumed her place behind the podium. Thomas listened attentively, working hard to hold back tears. His hands were bleeding onto his pants, but if he didn't move them too much, they started to clot.

"First, a short overview of what we will cover throughout the year," Mrs. Voss began. "While I am speaking, those in the back will sit quietly and listen attentively. This should all be review for Grays, but if any feel the need to take notes, you are not forbidden. We will start our lessons with something all here should already know.

"I need to ensure that you all fully understand where we came from. How we got where we are and what the Whites were forced to endure to get here. Your caregivers should have already provided this instruction, but in this class you will be tested on it. All lessons should be reviewed outside of class with your caregivers, so they can also be provided a fresh reminder of our shared history. If any caregivers do not want to join in your studies, they should be reported to the Grays. If any Color student misses a question, or says a wrong date, name, or pronoun, it will be met with swift and severe punishment. Because the Whites are gracious, a comprehensive summary will be provided before your tests.

"We will begin with history. The next few weeks will detail the most important dates, people, and events of our people's past. This information will be obvious to many of you, but, as we have just seen," Mrs. Voss looked up and directly at Isaiah, "there are some in this complex who continue to hate. Their caregivers have not taught the full and rich history of the Ascension, what led to it, and how pure and perfect our world is because of it.

"As we all know, the Whites were not always the gods we are now. Our ancestors were humans like you. During the Ascension, our ancestors became gods. Your ancestors, unfortunately," Mrs. Voss looked to the Grays and glanced at the Colors. She sighed before continuing, "your ancestors were not able to Ascend. So none of you are able to Ascend. This drove many of your ancestors to hate and punish and kill. We don't want that to be your fate. So we intervene, educate, and encourage that you may know what true and right worship is. Worship of Whites is the purest form, but we know there are those among you who turn their attention to lesser gods.

"Worship of lesser gods is allowed, even encouraged, so long as worship of the Whites is primary. The Whites are worshipped as a collected whole but the lesser gods of old were not worshipped that way. You will be taught the names and history of several of these gods, such as Baal, Dogan, and Azareal. These are gods from your history, gods your ancestors may have worshipped.

"There is one God that is not to be mentioned, however. A God who claimed to be the only God, though a triune at the same time. A God of separation and isolation. Believe it or not, but there are Colors living within these very walls that still worship this God." A White student in the front gasped loudly.

"I know," Mrs. Voss continued. "It's shocking to hear, but the Colors are weak. Colors are drawn by their very nature to this God. I dare not even speak his name for fear of stoking the darkness inside the hearts of the Colors in the back. There may be some among us who already know his name. They called themselves Christians, named after their God. Hate filled, blaspheming Christians are still with us today. Always watching, waiting, hiding in plain sight." Mrs. Voss had been staring at Isaiah but Thomas felt his body go cold as her malevolent stare passed over to him.

"But we Whites are merciful. We are brave and pure and good. We couldn't throw all Colors out because of the hatred of a few. For the sake of those Colors who want to try to be good, we Whites risk our lives and our safety in the presence of such hatred. We risk this to ensure those faithful to us are cared for.

"Before the Whites were able to Ascend, Christians hunted us down one by one. Christians murdered us in the streets. Killed us in our beds. Screamed, berated, attacked, and mocked. These monsters mocked the Whites for their goodness. The Whites were hated because we were willing to offer our love to anyone. We didn't recognize skin color, gender, age, sexual preference, birth bodies. The Whites believed that all people were one and should be loved as such. And even before our Ascension, the Whites recognized that we were good. Pure. Worthy of love and devotion, though not yet the worship of gods.

"But," Mrs. Voss let a dramatic pause hang in the air for a moment before continuing. "But, the Whites recognized that not all were good. There were some among them who were evil. Christians, for instance, who said we weren't all one, but were each alone. There was true evil in the world and it seemed to be embodied by Christians and their beliefs. Separated from their kin almost from birth, Christians saw people as sole individuals. They encouraged small, individual families instead of the far superior communal living we follow today. Well mostly." Mrs. Voss glared again at the Colors.

After a moment, she continued, "As I was saying. Christians saw themselves as individuals. Individuals who could act in their own self interest. Even to the extreme of hurting others for private gain. Christians would often try to silence others just for the color of their skin. Attack people because they just wanted to love who they loved. Mock those who weren't comfortable in their bodies and wanted to change them. The very things the Whites loved people for, Christians despised and attacked. Ridiculed and mocked.

"Christians had the hateful idea that humans were made to fill certain gender roles. Our bodies were made in just two types instead of the plethora we see today. Everyone living at that time was supposed to be either male or female. Man or woman. And once born, there was no changing it no matter how uncomfortable you might feel. Not only that, the genders each came with their own set of rules.

"If you were born into a woman's body, you were born to serve. Born to submit to a man and fulfill his every desire. You were not to have any agency of your own. If man, you were born to rule and dominate. Most of these horrible, hateful Christians were therefore men, though not all. Some women were willing to fight for their servitude. Fight to remain lesser and so their men could continue to dominate and control.

"Christian men saw themselves as the natural leaders of all people, though they did not see everyone as worthy of leading. The Whites of the day, who didn't want to follow the same hateful ideas were labeled as evil monsters. They were attacked and silenced. They were abandoned by the leaders and given zero support. The Whites, many of whom were unable to achieve positions of leadership, were attacked both physically and emotionally. Many Whites were murdered simply for disagreeing with the Christians who had seized positions of power.

"The descendents of those hateful people live among us today. The Colors all around you all had Christian grandparents. Men and women who decided that those not willing to think like them weren't worthy of life. So, the Whites were at the brink of complete and total annihilation. Until something changed. A spark lit.

"In cities all around the world, Whites started realizing their true nature. They were able to find their godhood. The Ascension began and the Whites began receiving the worship they were deserving of. This worship led to true followers and true change. Grays started bowing before the Whites, worshiping in any way they could. Some washed feet, some marched, some helped spread the message far and wide. Some were even willing to attack Christians and stop the hatred where it started. Many of the Grays in this room are descended from those who took up arms and fought. Killed Christians before they were able to kill the Whites.

"We owe these brave souls our gratitude. Without their support, the Whites would never have truly Ascended. Because the Ascension came at a cost. For the Ascension to be successful, all Whites had to give up their ability to cause physical harm to any. Whites became incapable of hurting others, which meant Christian monsters would be able to kill them with ease. Luckily, the Grays were there to protect them. And remain here to this day.

"The Whites and loyal Grays were relocated to a select few of the great cities. From here, our safety is ensured. They Grays protect and the Colors work to help support while the Whites do the greatest work of all and lead. This proper order ensures all are happy. All contribute meaningfully to the whole and all needs are met. We share all we have with the other great cities, ensuring all are fruitful and prosperous. The land between cities remains fallen and dangerous, hence our vast defensive wall.

"With the Ascension, the Whites were given great powers. We are able to communicate instantly between the great cities. We can move great distances through flight. We have gained knowledge to control even the sun." Mrs. Voss gestured at the light shining above the class. "This is an excellent example of how truly amazing and powerful the Whites are."

"But, despite our power, the Christian rebels are still a threat. The Whites have bestowed a great honor on the Colors: the honor of construction and maintenance for our mighty defensive wall. Very few rebels are capable of breaching it, ensuring protection for all. The rebels out there hate us. They hate the Whites, the Grays, but they hate the Colors in here most of all. The rebels see the Colors as traitors. Any Color caught out by the rebels is immediately killed for abandoning Christians during the Division War. We will get more into the specifics of that later, but the presence of Christian rebels just outside is a constant pull and temptation for the evil that still lives in the hearts of the Colors. No matter how much the rebels hate the Colors of this city, there are still many within these walls that dream of leaving here and joining their ranks. The Grays do a wonderful job monitoring for dissent among the Colors.

"The Grays also monitor for examples of selflessness demonstrated by the Colors. If noted, Colors can earn credits and even the possibility of earning their own Gray robes. While in this room, you Colors are here to demonstrate your true faith in the Whites. So, the Colors serve, the Grays protect and the Whites lead. All are giving to the betterment of our community. All are lead by Whites to be great people. People devoted to living with love, honesty, and godliness. By simply demonstrating faith and devotion, all peoples, no matter the color of their robes, all people are provided with food. With health care. With education. With housing. With jobs. All are provided everything they need to lead happy, productive lives. For All Are One."

"And One Serves All," the class echoed back.

The White let the room fill again with silence before continuing, "Now, that is a very broad history of our great people. Our great city. This will serve as a template for how we will continue your education. Colors, while you are listening quietly and attentively, I do want you to keep a few things in mind. You are evil. You are vile. You are descended from Christians who hated the Whites and did everything possible to kill us. Your ancestors, and therefore *you* if given the chance, would have hated me; hunted me; killed me, called me a man, he, him instead of my truth: they/them. They would have tried to wipe my very identity out of existence.

"The Christians would have hated Alicia here for her brave choice to love both Trifon *and* Pauline. They would have hated Trifon for loving Dante, simply because their skin isn't the same color but their gender expression is. They would have hated Pauline for her hair color, hated Dante because he didn't worship the same God as them. They would have found reasons to hate each White in this room. That hatred would have driven them to great evils: attacks, mocking, belittling, and even killing.

"These monsters are not far in your past, Colors. These were the parents of your parents. And these hateful traits pass down through blood. With enough work, some of you may be able to earn Gray robes, but many of you won't. Many of your parents still haven't shown enough decency and shame to earn their robes. So we know those hate filled beliefs are still rampant among you. And I need to ensure you know your place if I'm to help any of you rise above it."

The White let out a loud sigh and dropped her head. "Sometimes," she began after a moment. She let the room fill with silence again before continuing, "Sometimes I don't even know why I try. If all you are going to do is hate, why should I offer you my help? Why should we even spend the time with you, trying to show you a better way? A brighter way. All we ask is worship and we provide everyone with everything. Seems easy enough to me. But, every day you are here, your brightly colored clothing stands out. Brings attention to you and away from the purity of the Whites. Continues to prove that what we ask is too hard. Too much to ask." The White hung her head for almost a full minute before standing tall and pulling her shoulders back. The room waited in silence as she looked over the class.

"Now, the Great Division is generally accepted to have begun in 2013. In that time, a Christian man working as what was called a police officer, similar to our Grays now, shot a Seventeen year old boy for having some candy. Were he born today, that young man would have been a White. Were he not killed, that brave soul could have been Dante's grandfather." Mrs. Voss put a hand on Dante's shoulder. Thomas was surprised to see a tear fall on the table of one of the White students.

After a moment of silence, Mrs. Voss continued. "Large groups of people gathered to mourn the loss. Of course, more came when the Christian man walked free. After murdering a child in cold blood. No matter what story he tried to tell about being attacked, it could never warrant killing another human. Especially a good one. One who would have become a White.

"When an evil man kills a good kid, the only answer can be revenge. You don't benefit the world by allowing the evil back out. You do whatever you can to stop that evil once you know it's there. To ignore it means blood is on your hands. The next time that evil person kills someone, the blood is on your hands for seeing the evil and not stopping it. Unfortunately, for the Whites to truly see the evil, they lost the ability to stop it. Thankfully, a great many Grays were willing to stand up. Over the next few years, peaceful protests were burning through several major cities all across the world."

The White continued for the rest of the day, listing protest after protest. There were also several names of Whites killed by evil Christians that fueled more protests. Thomas listened attentively, trying to learn the names. The pain in his hands was intense and he was willing to try anything to distract himself.

CHAPTER 6

L ily stood in the narrow hall, having just said goodbye to Thomas.
 She watched as the door closed slowly. When it finally shut, she
let out a sigh and turned. She could feel the fear for him rising. She
felt helpless. She did the only thing she could think to do, she prayed.
She begged God to watch over Thomas, to give him strength and
courage. She felt her fear dissipate slightly and a small smile cross her
lips as she reached the door to her classroom.

She took her usual seat in the back of the room. Then she turned
her eyes to the front door, waiting. She felt her pulse rise each time
the door opened. Finally, she saw him. Craig. He froze for a second,
making eye contact with her. She watched a small smile start in his
eyes and then continue to his mouth. He jumped when he realized
someone was waiting in the door behind him. Lily watched as Craig
looked down and quickly made his way toward his desk, another
Gray following close behind.

Lily watched in shock as Craig walked past his desk. He was
walking right toward her. He kept his eyes down as he walked quickly.
He rounded the back row of desks and passed right in front of her.
Lily felt the leg of her pant shift as he brushed against her. Once
past, Craig quickly walked up the next row and sat in his seat. He
had never done that before. He had barely acknowledged her with
anything more than a smile like she'd seen today. She felt a connec-
tion between them, but was shocked he was willing to risk so much
attention to walk to the back of the class like that.

Just when she was calming down, she saw a small paper on the
ground in front of her. She quickly glanced up at the Gray guard

in front of the room. He was looking out the window, probably watching for the White. She put her foot over the note and slid it back. She held perfectly still for a moment, not daring to draw any attention to herself. The Colors on either side of her didn't seem to have noticed anything. They were sitting silently with their heads bowed. Lily could see the blank stare common in so many Colors. Her dad said it was the Sacrament they were given after Worship, but Lily wasn't sure. Either way, her family never ate the Sacrament but instead flushed it when they got home.

After a full minute not moving, Lily finally felt calm enough to do something. She used one foot to pull the shoe off her other foot. She put an annoyed look on her face and bent down to adjust her shoe. She felt like she was being unnecessarily dramatic, but she couldn't stop herself. Her heart was racing as she grabbed the small note, placed it in her shoe, and then put her shoe back on her foot.

She smiled to herself and glanced at Craig, wishing she could get his attention. She wanted to let him know she'd gotten the note but there was no way. Lily smiled to herself, thinking about how nice it was going to be to feel that note throughout the remainder of the class period. Lily worked hard to keep herself from smiling as the rest of the class filed in. The Grays stood as the Whites entered.

Lily watched through the hair hanging in front of her face as an overweight woman walked into the room. Lily felt her stomach fill with disgust as she watched the woman walk. *I wonder if she'd roll if she fell.* Lily felt the thought come unbidden to her mind. She immediately regretted it. First, it was unkind and she felt guilty. But second, the idea of this woman rolling around on the floor was really funny. Lily almost started to laugh and had to bite her tongue to stop herself. Then she felt more guilt.

The woman finally stepped up to the podium. She used the hem of her sleeve to dab her forehead. She took a deep breath and then looked to the class. "Welcome class to your final year. By the end of this year, your general education will be completed. Any not continuing on," the White paused for a moment, surveying the Colors sitting in the back of the class, "…will be given a work assignment by the end of the year. Today we begin a series of lessons to ensure you have an adequate understanding of how our economic system works. This will allow you all to contribute most effectively to our society.

"I am aware that many in this class will have never even heard the word economics. This is the system of ownership that allows our society to function. The work assignments and credit system the Whites have implemented to ensure all contribute for the good of our city as a whole. Many of you spent your early years in the Care Center and have since been in school. Because of this, you have not been expected to contribute to our society. That will change soon. Upon graduation this year, you will be expected to contribute where you are most needed. You will also be expected to contribute as much as you can.

"The how and why of Creditism will be taught to you over the course of the entire year, but we will start today with a basic overview. Before we can truly begin, we need to go back. Prior to the Ascension most people in the world were stifled by what was called capitalism. This was an economic system derived entirely around the love of money and the love of self.

"I know it can be difficult for us to appreciate, living enlightened and without money as we do, but money was central to almost everything in the old world. You needed money for food, for clothing, for water. Without money you couldn't communicate, couldn't sleep. You couldn't even receive healthcare without money. How did people get this money? They were born into it.

"If you weren't born into a family with money, it was almost impossible to get any of your own. Supporters of the system spread a lie that anyone could work their way up, but this simply was not possible. They even made up a lie of a phrase to describe it. *Lift yourself by your bootstraps* they would say, an impossible task for anyone. But they didn't care. They didn't care for any not born wealthy. Didn't care how hard life was without money. Didn't care about anyone but themselves. And who were those perpetuating this lie? Christians, of course." The White paused here for a moment, glaring at the back of the classroom.

"Eventually," she continued, "when enough people realized how flawed this system was, a few brave people spoke up against it. Some, though not all, of these people later Ascended. Those who were willing to focus on the material needs of the common man became ancestors of the Whites you know today. Only when the power grabbing, controlling, evil system of capitalism was destroyed could the system we have in place today thrive.

"Instead of working for oneself, people began working for the good of all. For All Are One." The White stopped her speech for a moment while the room replied, "And One Serves All." The White looked pleasingly around the room at the quick response. She took a breath and continued.

"Today all have jobs. All are given equal pay for equal work and everyone contributes their efforts toward a common good. If anyone is willing to go above and beyond, they are given extra credits to purchase something special for themselves. But, a common minimum is given by all to the benefit and safety of all. This minimum work provides all people with enough food, clothing, water, shelter, and health care. Basic amenities every person deserves.

"Of course, our system isn't perfect." She stared toward the back of the room, moving her eyes along each Color student sitting in the back. "There are those among us who are not willing to contribute their fair share. There will, of course, always be those who are lazy. Those who are selfish. Those not wanting to help others and only wanting to do enough for themselves. Grays and Whites, I'd like you to stand and turn, facing the Colors around the room."

Noise rang out as the students stood. Once they were facing the Colors, the White said, "Those not willing to help are sitting in the back. The Colors have always been lazy and unwilling. Fortunately for us, the Grays are very attentive. They monitor the work to ensure each Color is putting in their fair share of effort. If any are caught not contributing, they are punished immediately. A second offense is a public whipping and a third could be seen as treason. Treason against the city and blasphemy against the Whites. What do you think a fitting punishment for such a crime should be?"

"Death," was heard almost immediately from one of the White students. Lily didn't look up to see who spoke, but felt a chill run down her spine at the sound of such a wicked tone coming from a child's mouth. A child the same age as her.

"Correct," the White said. "You may sit." When all the class was sitting and paying attention again, the White continued, "so, always be on guard. Our system only works if all are contributing. All are giving what they are able to the common pool. Then we all prosper. Any shortcomings and we are all shorted. Now, who specifically devised this amazing system? Over the next few weeks we will learn of its inception, the attacks on Creditism by Christians throughout history, and how capitalism eventually devoured itself and gave rise to Creditism.

"In 2024, a great and powerful leader who identified as a woman named Alex Andra O-" Lily felt her attention drifting. The rest of the day passed quickly for Lily. She didn't learn much but she had been watching Craig all day, praying that he would turn around again and look at her. Lily didn't know how she could tell, but she could feel him actively looking away from her all day. Finally, the last bell rang. The Whites stood up and filed out of the room. When they had cleared the building, the Gray guard motioned for the Grays to leave.

They filed out in their usual, orderly fashion. The Color students kept their eyes averted, in the normal respectful pose for Grays. Lily knew she shouldn't look but she couldn't help herself. She glanced at Craig just as he glanced at her. Their eyes met and they each smiled. He quickly looked away, but Lily noticed a slight redness flare up on his cheeks. He continued walking to the door, saluting the guard on his way out. Lily couldn't help but watch, praying for another glance. As soon as Craig was out of sight, the guard looked straight at Lily. He gave her a knowing smile and a nod before returning the salute of the next Gray.

Lily felt her stomach drop at the look in the guard's eye. She quickly dropped her eyes to the ground, waiting for the final bell to indicate they could leave. She felt her heart racing, wondering what the guard had seen. He had noticed something, and Lily was getting panicked about what that meant. She jumped out of her chair as the sound of the bell rang out, indicating the Color students could leave.

She darted to the door, trying to get out first so she could meet Thomas and he wouldn't have to wait alone. In her hurry, she forgot about her worries for a second. She rushed down the hall and waited at the back door to his classroom. The door was open and kids were already moving out, heads down as they trudged through the dark, dirty hallway.

Lily tried to stand out of the way, allowing other students to pass, but there was no room for kids to move around her. She was already holding up traffic. She called into the room, "Thomas, I'll meet you outside!" She thought she heard his response, but couldn't be sure. *Worst case, I can just come in when the rest of the kids are out* she thought to herself as she walked out of the building.

Her mind had returned to the look on the guard's face while she waited for Thomas. She stood along the fence, watching students leave one by one. The flow of kids stopped and the door closed. She hadn't seen Thomas yet. She was just about to open the door, when it opened toward her. Thomas came out, holding bloody hands in front of himself.

Lily jumped into action. The blood had dried, leaving a dark brown stain to his hands. She sat Thomas on the ground, his back pressed against the fence. She examined his hands closely and was glad to see that the cuts didn't appear to be near as bad as they looked at first. The wounds were scabbed closed and none were frighteningly deep. At least the bleeding had stopped.

"Must have happened earlier today?" Lily asked Thomas who was grimacing in pain. He did seem more in control now that his hands were clean. He was obviously in pain but was trying to hide it. Lily smiled at the silliness of that but listened as he responded.

"Yeah, it was first thing this morning," Thomas said. He squeezed his fingers and one of the scabs right over his knuckle broke open and started bleeding. The blood splashed off the dirt and onto the fence.

"Hey, take care of that!" the guard yelled. Lily nodded quickly and took off her shoe.

"What are you doing?" Thomas asked surprised.

Lily took off her sock before turning to her brother. "We gotta cover that bleeding. The Whites would not be happy if Color blood were spilled on their street." Thomas nodded to himself as he allowed Lily to wrap his hand.

She smiled to herself when she finished and put her shoe back on. Her stomach dropped when she realized that she couldn't feel the note anymore. She quickly scanned the ground and saw it lying near the fence. She watched in horror as a Gray reached his fingers through the fence and grabbed the note. He met her eyes and smiled. It was the same guard from her classroom.

He pulled the note through the fence and opened it. He smiled to himself then looked back to Lily. He shook his head and then turned and left, dropping the note on the ground. Lily finally got to see what Craig had given her. It was a small but beautifully drawn picture of a sun. Lily wasn't sure what it meant, but it stirred something in her. She was impressed with the details and the quality of the drawing. She looked at it one more time, very saddened that it was just out of her reach. She put her arm around Thomas's shoulder and started walking home.

CHAPTER 7

G race tried to keep herself from panicking. She had been told to go after noon, but had no idea what that meant. She had been praying, but felt like the usual comforting, calming voice of God was being yanked away from her again and again. She was distracted by the thought of Connors's eyes. That image thrust itself into her mind every time she tried to pray. It was exhausting and she felt her fear rising.

She looked to her left again. The sun was shining onto the wall on her left through windows high above her. She had chosen a random poster (THE WHITES NEED YOU!) and decided that, when the sun first touched that poster, she would leave. The poster was almost fully sunlit. Grace couldn't force herself to go. She looked down and realized she had completed her assignment.

After watering the plants, she had been tasked with cleaning out old pots to make room for something new. She had completed all of the pots. She looked up again, knowing that she had no other options. She needed to alert a Gray that her task was completed so she could be given the necessary materials for a new task. She also knew that she couldn't ignore her assignment to Connors any longer. She felt the hunger in her stomach be replaced by nausea as she turned and held up her arm.

The Gray who had been escorting her throughout the day saw her hand up and came to her table. "Do you need help with something?" he asked. His tone was more gentle than she was used to and she was grateful for the familiar face.

"Yes, sir," Grace replied, keeping her gaze away from the man's face. "I was told by a White to be escorted to the Tower after noon today."

"Yeah, I remember," the Gray replied. "I suppose you want me to take you?" Grace didn't reply but kept her head down and kept silent, unsure what to say. The man sighed and then stood a little taller. "Alright, follow me."

He started off at a brisk pace. Grace followed close behind but tried to stay out of the way. They walked up to an older Gray standing at the door. His gaze swept back and forth around the room, his hand on his gun. The young man Grace was following stopped a few feet away from the older man and stood at attention, feet together and hand on his forehead, waiting to be acknowledged.

The older man ignored them for a minute longer before saying, "What is it private?"

"Sir," the younger man replied, maintaining his pose, "White Connors instructed this Color to report to the Tower after noon today. Shall I escort her?"

The older man grunted in response. "You tryin' to get outta' duty, private?"

"No, sir," Grace's escort replied quickly. "It's just someone needs to do it and I don't want to put the burden on any others, sir."

The older man grunted again. Grace remained still. She always tried to maintain a posture of submission but had learned how to watch her superiors. After a moment, the older man stood from his seat and stepped close to the young man. Grace felt a chill as the captain's gaze swept up and down her body.

"Private Gates, that right?" the older man said, looking at the young man's uniform. "I'll be watching for you Gates. It should only take a few minutes to get to the Tower, I expect you back here before fourteen hundred to resume your post."

The young man's shoulders dropped slightly for a second, but then he stood tall again, finished his salute, and turned to the door. They rushed out of the building and into the bright day. Not even taking a few seconds to let their vision adjust to the daylight, Gates began marching quickly down the paved street. Grace almost had to run to keep up with him.

They turned a corner and Grace stopped. She looked straight ahead, trying to take it all in. Her eyes were drawn up the large, White walls of the Tower. It was still a few blocks ahead but it was by far the largest building Grace had ever seen. If she had stacked her shack on itself four times, it still probably wouldn't be as tall as the Tower. The sides were a mix of White walls and black windows. Grace was curious to see the strange lines running from the top of the building and down the sides.

She jumped when Private Gates whistled. She nodded and then started jogging, catching up with the young man. She passed several shops as they approached the inner fence but most of the buildings around her appeared empty. She counted four open doors and only a few Grays milling around. Grace and Private Gates were ignored by all they saw. Grace watched a Gray turn the corner, see them coming, and immediately cross to the other side of the street.

After a few minutes of silent racing, they made it to the gate. Two Grays stood at the gate, monitoring all who passed. Their backs were turned from the Tower and facing the street. Grace kept her head bowed as Private Gates stood attention. "Private Gates, here," he said loudly.

"Yes, Private Gates," the man on the left replied. "Sergeants Jones and Faber. Assume the position."

Private Gates finished his salute and then dropped to his knees. Grace followed and noticed that the paved road was painted white in front of her. Private Gates solemnly leaned forward and kissed the white pavement. Grace, unsure what to do, followed his lead.

Her head barely started to drop when she felt a sharp jab in her lower back. "No!" Sergeant Jones yelled out. "Colors do not sully the pavement of the Whites. Keep your filthy lips off the sacred ground." She felt her body go stiff, as well as the body of Private Gates next to her.

A moment of silence hung on the air. Grace wasn't sure what to say but kept perfectly still. Gates's voice broke the silence stating, "My apologies, sir. I should have provided her with clearer instructions."

The guards remained quiet for a moment. Grace held her breath, waiting for a response. Finally Jones replied, "We expect better next time, private. On with your business. Who are you to see?"

Private Gates stood, pulling gently on Grace's arm. He moved her behind him and she assumed the normal position, head bowed in respect of her superiors. Private Gates stood tall with his shoulders back and chin thrust forward. "Your honor, this woman has been instructed by White Connors to report to zim's chambers."

Grace kept an eye on all of the men as they talked. She didn't think they noticed her watching, but couldn't be sure. Private Gates stood at respect, Sergeant Jones seemed aloof, but Sergeant Faber frightened her. She watched as Faber's eyes tracked down and then back up her body. He had a hungry look on his face and barely seemed to be listening to the other two.

"Of course," Jones said. "Be on your way. For All Are One."

"And One Serves All, sir," Private Gates repeated, before finishing his salute. He then reached around the corner of the gate and into a small box at about waist height. Grace had no idea what he was doing. After a moment, he pulled his hand back with a small stack of blue paper. Grace was even more confused as Private Gates began removing his shoes. He noticed she was just standing there and nodded to her, motioning to her shoes.

Grace watched as Private Gates took his shoe off, held his foot above the ground, unfolded the blue paper, which Grace realized was an oversized, plastic sock, put his foot in the sock, and set his foot down on the white pavement. If things weren't so tense, Grace would have found the entire maneuver funny. She sighed and then followed, removing her shoes and putting on the new socks in the same manner.

They were both about to leave the gate when Faber's voice called out, "Hold it." Grace felt herself freeze. "What about her clothes?" Faber finished.

Grace's eyes snapped up and met the man's. He gave her a lecherous smile. Grace quickly dropped her eyes to the ground, realizing she would have no choice but to do what the men said. She prayed to God for protection and listened as the men continued talking.

"What of them," Jones replied.

"Well, those are filthy, sir," Faber said. "Do you think she should bring that mess into the White complex? I think it might be best if she stripped." Grace could hear lust in his voice.

"Ugh," Jones replied, "and be forced to see her naked? You may want to see a dirty Color body but I don't and I don't think the Whites would appreciate it either."

Grace watched in surprise as Faber's shoulders deflated slightly. Grace could see the age difference between the two guards for the first time. Faber was much younger than Jones and seemed to be trying to earn his approval. "No sir," Faber replied, motioning quickly to her legs. "Look how close to the ground they are. If she drags dirt in, it may upset the Whites." He looked somewhat pleadingly to Jones, awaiting a response.

Jones made a show of examining her pant legs. "Yes, I see what you mean," Jones replied after a moment. "You are correct, the pants and shirt should be removed, but no more."

Faber nodded respectfully and then turned an evil smile back on Grace. She kept her gaze down and finished her prayer, first thanking God that she didn't have to get naked, and then begging for strength. She began removing her pants. They untied at the waist and dropped over her thin legs, leaving only a pair of dirty orange shorts and the blue, paper socks. The irony of removing her pants because they might get the white pavement dirty, then dropping them directly on that white pavement struck her as odd. She pulled her oversized shirt off, exposing her body to the men. She smiled when she realized that God had helped her wear a tank top today.

Once her clothes were off, Private Gates quickly started walking away from the guards. Grace followed but gave one last glance through her hair toward Faber. She was careful not to make eye contact and tried not be noticed. He continued leering at her body for a moment longer, but then turned back to the street, resuming his post. Grace turned her attention to Private Gates's back, but felt her eyes drawn up the sides of the enormous building.

Now that she was closer, she could see that the black lines were cords like she had seen in the Garden. She also saw several ugly, gray boxes jutting out the sides of the building through windows in seemingly random spots. The closer they got, the less intimidating it was. She looked at the ground around her instead.

They walked along a narrow white path cutting through a large, green field of grass. A short distance away, she could see another narrow path leading to a separate gate in the fence. They passed a large tree and Grace almost stopped when she noticed fruit growing from it. She couldn't remember having tasted an apple before but had picked them from the Orchard when she was a child working with her mother. A large part of her wanted to rush over to taste the fruit, but she knew that it would be deadly.

They rushed along the path and arrived at a glass door. A small, black tablet was attached to the wall next to the door. Private Gates pressed his thumb on it, causing the tablet to light up. Grace was shocked but was able to read list of names over the man's shoulder. Connors was one of the first names, preceded by Altman and Anderson. Gates pressed firmly on Connors's name and the screen went blank for a second.

Then Grace watched in awe as the screen came to life, with Connors's face on it. He coughed and rubbed his eyes then gave them a confused, distant look. "Who's that?"

"Holy Connors," Private Gates said to the screen. "It is my honor to be in your presence and to serve you. I have brought the Color woman you requested from the Gardens."

Connors looked into the screen in silence for a moment, watching Private Gates. He slowly blinked and shook his head as he said, "I don't remember. Let me see her."

Private Gates nodded and then pulled Grace into the place he had just been standing. Grace felt like she was staring straight at Connors, and didn't know where to look. She would usually keep her gaze down, but felt that would be disrespectful. She gazed straight into his eyes for what felt like a very long moment. Connors stared back at her, then recognition filled his face as he smiled. Grace felt a small chill at that smile.

"Oh, right," he said. "Her. Yes, you may send her in."

"Thank you, your holiness. For All Are One."

"And One Serves All," Connors replied.

The screen went blank and a loud buzzing noise filled the air. Grace jumped at the sound but Private Gates seemed to be expecting it. He pulled on the door and pushed her into the building. Grace looked back through the glass as the door clicked shut. Private Gates met her eyes and then motioned behind her. He mouthed *go* before turning and walking away.

Grace turned slowly and stared down a long, bright hallway. Every surface she could see was white. The walls painted, the floor a bright, shiny stone. However, she could also see several spots along the walls and floor that appeared to be stained with dark brown smudges. She made her way down the hall, avoiding the sticky surfaces.

On either side of her, the white walls were lit with electric lights. She had nowhere to go but forward. The hallway ended with a white wall and a single, closed, shining golden door. Grace noticed a crack in the middle of the door and stepped closer. She almost yelled out as the door separated along the crack and a bell rang out. On the other side of the golden door, was a small room with glass walls. On the other side of the glass was another world.

Grace felt her jaw drop as she stared into a beautiful forest filled with trees bearing fruit of all kinds. Grace could never imagine a forest growing inside of a building, but as she glanced up, she could see the sky. She followed the lines of the building around her and realized there was a hole in the center of the building. She also noticed several people dressed in White robes holding white railings along the inside edge of the building. Everyone she saw seemed to be watching her.

Grace was barely able to keep herself from jumping as the bell rang out and the door slid shut. She wasn't, however, able to stop the whimper that passed her lips when the room started moving. She watched as the room climbed up the length of all the trees surrounding her. She tried not to stare at the Whites but could not keep her eyes off the view out the window. When she passed the tree line, she was able to see the open room in its entirety.

There were other rooms like hers along the interior walls. Each room seemed to be contained with a glass shaft. Along the bottom of the shaft was a small grove of trees, the one she just passed through.

Between the groves were large, open paths of white, similar to the path her and Private Gates had just used. In the center of the opening, was a large lake. A small area of yellow dirt surrounded lake.

Grace's eyes quickly took a count of the Whites in the room. Aside from the seven she'd already counted watching her along the walls, she also saw two walking slowly along the path and another pair swimming in the water. The water was bluer than anything Grace had ever seen, and so clear she could see the dark skin of the Whites through the water.

The bell dinged again and the room stopped moving. Grace could see there was still one level above her. She felt a tremble of fear wash over her body at the realization that there were entire buildings standing on top of her. The wall slid apart again and Grace froze. Connors stood just on the other side, smiling.

CHAPTER 8

"Welcome, my dear," Connors said with a smile and a gentle tone. Grace felt her heart racing alongside her mind as she tried to figure out what was happening. Her eyes swept over the room as she stepped through the doors. The shock of the room drew her attention away from Connors momentarily. She saw more stains like the hall behind her. She also saw a mess of garbage piled along the edges of the room. There was white furniture and a lot of light, but also a lot of random stuff lying around in the house. She saw robes, dishes, pills similar to the Sacrament, and a lot of items she didn't recognize.

Grace was brought back to the moment by the sound of a light bell ring out behind her. She realized the doors had closed behind her. She was truly alone with the man who stood in front of her, analyzing her every move. Grace took a deep breath and began dropping to the pose of worship. She stopped breathing as her movement was cut short.

A firm, steady pressure on her chin made her freeze. From above, Connors said, "No, no. None of that. Not here. Not now." His falsely high pitched, effeminate voice sent a chill down Grace's spine. Grace followed as Connors used pressure from his cane to pull her to her feet.

He stared straight into her eyes. She wasn't able to do anything but stare back. He breathed slowly, moving his face forward until he was just inches from hers. He stared deeply into her eyes but didn't say a word. He almost seemed to be holding his breath now. Grace could feel his malicious intent but couldn't figure out what he wanted. A full minute passed in silence as Grace could only stare back into Connors's eyes. A minute of discomfort and torture.

In her mind, Grace imagined a knife stabbing into her chest. A hammer slamming into her head. Or even just his fists. As she thought of all the things Connors could do, she found herself naturally starting a silent prayer to God begging for strength. As always, she felt a gentle relaxing in her chest. She calmed slightly.

She jumped as Connors yelled out triumphantly, "Aha!" Grace stepped back and dropped her gaze. She was relieved to move her eyes away from his, but felt a rising terror in her chest. She listened as he continued, "I knew it!" Connors looked around one more time before saying to her, almost in a whisper, "You're a believer, aren't you?"

Grace felt her heart drop. How could he know? She ran through their interactions and realized he had seen her pray both times. Watched her to see what she would do when stressed. She dropped to her knees, placing her head on the ground. She sat there silently, knowing what he was going to ask next.

She had seen it for herself several times, but it had been years. She couldn't even remember the last accusation. While she was on the ground, her mind raced through the Trials. A Color would be accused by a peer or a Gray of being a believer. Grays could be accused too, but that didn't happen often. Once accused, an assembly would immediately be called of all those living in the district. Once all were gathered, the accused would face a White directly. The accused then had two choices.

They could state publicly for all to hear: "I pledge my belief in the Whites. They are my gods and I worship them as gods. I pray for mercy and understanding from the Whites and will work to earn their forgiveness and love. I deny the divinity of Jesus Christ." Then, a White would use a metal brand to burn "666" on the right hand of the accused.

The other option was to denounce the Whites as god, in which case the accused would be beheaded by a Gray. No one took this option. In the history of the Complex, not a single individual had stood up for God, which Grace found somewhat saddening.

Grace lay with her face pressed to the ground in silence, waiting. And she prayed. She prayed to God for strength, for courage, that He watch over Rhys and Lily and Thomas. She prayed as hard as she could that God would have mercy on her and welcome her into His loving embrace. She thanked Jesus for her salvation and prayed that she would be able to watch over her family from heaven. Grace was convinced she was about to die.

She found herself wondering what the blade would feel like against her neck. At that thought, she realized nothing had happened for a long time. Connors stood silently above her. Grace opened her eyes and tried to look around the room. Connors must have seen her moving because as soon as she shifted he said, "You done?"

Grace wasn't sure how to answer. She replied, speaking into the floor, "Yes, your holiness."

"Great!" Connors replied. He grabbed her by the arm pulled her up. She stood tall and realized that she was taller than him. She looked down at him as he started talking quietly. "Now, I want you to look at me."

He stepped back and half sat against the side of his couch. Connors looked at her for a moment, as if to make sure she was paying attention. When he was satisfied he nodded and said, "You are aware of what you are and what I could do to you?" Grace nodded. "Good. So you know that I now rule over your entire life at this point, right?" Grace nodded, again. "You know that I could ask you to do anything, ask anyone to do anything to you, and it would be done?" Grace nodded, but felt sure there were a few things she wouldn't do. "Ok, so your life is in my hands. How does that not make me your god?"

Grace was stunned. She stared in silence, unable to come up with any words. She opened and closed her mouth a few times, but nothing came out. She couldn't make her mind work. Connors became irritated. "Ok," Connors continued, "let's try something else. Right now, I want you to talk to me. I want to hear your complete, full thoughts and beliefs. If you do not answer, you will be killed. If I feel you are not being completely honest, you will be killed. I want full, truthful answers and nothing less. Now, why do you not consider me your god? Or at least *A* god of yours?"

Grace stared at the strange man in front of her. His hair was long on one side of his face, but shaved short on the other. He had died it a pink color but it was fading. His skin still looked clammy and almost had a sickly color to it. Grace felt herself become nauseous. She turned her attention away from his body and to the words he had said. She thought: *why not? He's right, what have I got to lose?* She took a deep breath, prayed that the Holy Spirit would guide her tongue, and then started. "Because you are not God. Not *A* god. You are a man."

Grace watched Connors close his eyes as if he had been physically struck at the word 'man.' He kept them closed for a moment and Grace worried she had gone too far. Had she made him angry enough to have her killed already? After a moment he composed himself and looked to her. She could see the anger in his eyes as he replied, "Wrong. But, even if I am just human, I am a zir in complete control of you. One of many anyways. How is that any different from a god?"

"God is not control. God is the opposite of control. God is freedom. Freedom to choose to follow, choose to worship, choose to die for. You cannot gain that reverence by force."

Connors looked thoughtfully at her for a second. "Good answer," he finally replied. "That's not one I've heard before. I like that one. So you're saying what we might be missing is freedom. But what of those that choose not to worship? Shouldn't they be killed for turning away?"

Grace got the feeling he was half talking to himself. She didn't want to interrupt, but couldn't stop herself as she said, "Killed for not liking you?" The carelessness in Connors's voice caused a chill to run down her spine.

"Well they don't have to like us, but they do have to worship. And if we just killed any that didn't worship, there wouldn't really be a choice, huh?" Connors looked expectantly to Grace and asked, "So, what does your God do for you?"

Grace started slowly and quietly as she replied, "He shows me the way. He gives me peace, comfort, and joy, along with all of the other true fruits; the fruits of the spirit. He gives me a way to live in this broken world with hope and forgiveness. He gives me courage and reminds me that suffering can be borne well and can lead to beautiful things if done correctly. He gives me the strength to bring even tiny amounts of light to this dark world." By the end of the sentence, she was speaking loudly and confidently. She never thought she'd have the courage to speak to a White like this, but felt like she was being given the words. She smiled as she realized her prayer for help from the Holy Spirit had been answered.

Connors stared at her for a moment. "Yeah, I can't compete with that, can I?" He shook his head then stood and said, "But can your God do this?" He leaped toward Grace, grabbing her arm and pulling her body against his. He pressed his lips against hers, aggressively. She felt a wave of revulsion at the rough, dry feeling of his lips against hers. She pulled away from him as far as she could, but he had his arm around her, holding her in place. She wasn't strong enough to break free.

"Playing coy?" he asked with a smile. "I know you like it, otherwise I wouldn't be able to do it."

He must have read the confusion in Grace's eyes, because he continued, "You're confused? As a White I cannot cause pain to anyone. So, if you were not interested, I wouldn't be able to hold you like this. A part of you must want me to be doing this or I wouldn't physically be capable of doing it. And I'm enjoying it too." He placed a hand behind her head and pulled her face against his again.

Grace didn't think, just reacted. She felt her teeth close over his lip. She bit as hard as she could for just a moment before she realized what she'd done. Connors squeaked and jumped back. He let her go with one arm and pushed her away with his other. He had a hand over his mouth as he stared at her, an almost gleeful look in his eyes. Grace could see the excitement barely covering a look of malevolence.

Connors stared silently at her. After a few seconds, he stood taller and straightened his robes. He pulled his hand back from his lip and looked at a small dab of blood on his finger. He held eye contact with Grace as he licked the blood from his lip.

He finally said, "Well, thank you for your time. I think that's everything." At that, he pulled out a gun from his waist and grabbed a knife off the table. "So, which will it be? Bullet or blade?"

Grace stared in horror, unsure how to answer. "Your grace, please…"

"Why are you begging me?" Connors asked with a smirk. "Shouldn't you be talking to your God?"

Grace closed her eyes and prayed. Connors watched her in silence and said, "Whoa! My mind is changed! It worked! I see your value now and will allow you to put on my White robes and take my place in honor. Your God has convinced me so." Grace opened her eyes. Connors was bent forward in an exaggerated laugh. Grace could see the fat rolls on his stomach jiggling and felt that nausea return.

"No, I'm just kidding," he said when he'd composed himself. "I can't hurt you anyways, remember? But, I do have a job for you." Grace watched as Connors set down the gun and the knife and leaned back against the couch again. Once he was comfortable, he continued, "Nothing difficult. Nothing major. You won't have to hurt anyone or anything like that. I just need you to grow a plant for me. Something you already do, right?"

Grace's mind was racing. She knew she couldn't trust him, but couldn't think of any way to respond. "What plant?" she asked after a minute.

"Nightshade," Connors replied with a dark smile. "The White in control of your Garden has threatened me. I cannot allow this to stand. His daughter purchases tea from the shop supplied by your Garden. The tea she normally drinks will be replaced with Nightshade. All you have to do is plant some seeds and water a plant for about two weeks. The rest will be done by others."

Grace didn't know what to say. She stood shocked and terrified at the plan developed by the monster in front of her. He seemed to take her silence as agreement and said, "I'll send a Gray with the seeds when the time is right. It should be soon, but we'll have to be careful. Don't want you getting caught. That could raise some questions about me and that would be very bad for you. Also know that, if you don't follow my instructions, I'll have you killed, obviously. But not just you, your entire family."

Grace couldn't respond, but only stared in shocked silence at what she was being asked to do. And who she was being asked by. "Great!" he replied with a smile. "Should I call us partners then?" he winked at her as he used his cane to push a button on the wall behind her. The same small bell rang and the wall opened behind her once again. Grace stepped silently into the small room, her mind racing.

"Better hurry back," Connors replied. "Your White will be wondering where you are."

Grace was shocked to realize that he hadn't done anything to cover for her absence. She bolted out of the elevator as soon as it opened and ran as fast as she could back to her Garden, tears running down her face. She could still feel the pressure of his lips against hers and was proud that she only had to stop once to vomit.

CHAPTER 9

———— ❦ ————

"**H**e what?!" Rhys almost yelled.

"Quiet," Grace replied and put her finger to her lip. She motioned toward the bedroom where the kids were getting ready for Worship. Rhys and Grace stood in their kitchen, alone. She had just filled him in on what Connors had done. "I don't want to worry the kids."

"He what?!" Rhys repeated in a whisper. Grace noticed his cheeks filling with blood. He was really angry. Grace stepped closer and put her arms around Rhys's shoulders.

She put her head against his chest and said, "It's over. I'm fine. What he did to me isn't important, it's what he wants me to do." She was hoping to gloss over the kiss, which was terrible but in the past and couldn't be changed. She wanted Rhys to help her focus on the poisoning Connors wanted her to help with. She knew she could never bring herself to do that. Not even be a part of it. She was willing to lay down her own life before helping kill a child, but what of her family's life? She was panicking and needed Rhys to help calm her down.

"Uh, it's a big deal to me." Rhys continued, but Grace could feel him trying to let it go. He sighed and pressed his lips against the top of her head. They held each other silently for a moment, neither of them speaking. This had always been how they'd supported each other when things got stressful. Holding each other centered them and reminded each of them what really matters. It had always helped calm things down and was a great way to remind each other that they were on the same team. That they were supposed to fight together against the Devil, not against each other.

They rocked like that for a while, just enjoying the feeling of each other's presence. Grace could feel Rhys relaxing into her, which helped her relax into him. Some of her stress melted away. When they separated, they were both much calmer.

Grace started, "I know, what he did to me was a big deal. I get that. But it's done and it is over now. There are bigger things to worry about."

Rhys took a deep breath, as he stepped back. He ran his hand through his short beard as he gazed at nothing and thought. Grace kept quiet, knowing he liked to work things out in his head first. All of a sudden he jumped in place a few times and shook his arms, catching Grace off guard. In her surprise she felt more tension leave her body.

"Right," Rhys said, "OK. So, what do we do? You obviously can't grow that for him." Grace was so relieved to hear him say those words. A part of her was worried he was going to tell her to do it. Tell her there was no other way. Give her permission to do something evil. She didn't know it before, but hearing his words closed a door in her mind. Following the plan was no longer even a possibility to her.

"So, what do we do? You can't ignore him either," Rhys continued. He was looking around the room, as if trying to find the answer. Like he'd dropped it somewhere. Grace started chuckling to herself, partly in emotional shock from the roller coaster of these last few minutes, and partly because she was so relieved to have her husband. The laughter started rolling out of her, stopping her from speaking all together.

Rhys stared at his wife before he started chuckling too. "Something funny?" he asked.

After Grace composed herself slightly, she said, "You think you're gonna find a note on the floor? Something from God saying: 'Hi, these two are under my protection, please forget all plans previously made and have a nice day'?"

Grace fell into another fit of quiet laughter. Rhys chuckled at her and then replied, "You never know. Moses heard a bush right?

Who's to say it couldn't be our table? Or the sink drain? But you've got a point, God *is* watching over us, isn't he?"

Grace came to herself and nodded in response. Smiling at the faith of her husband. She stepped toward him and pulled him into a gentle kiss. For a second she felt the nausea start again as she remembered Connors's lips on hers, but all that was washed away when Rhys returned the kiss. He held her lovingly, passionately, and with strong, supportive arms. She felt herself leaning into his muscular frame. It felt like leaning into a rock. Her worries evaporated completely as he held her.

After a long kiss, Grace put her head against Rhys's shoulder. "Then that's what we'll do. That's all we can do. Pray and trust God." Grace looked up at him, gave Rhys a small kiss. It was her turn to surprise him. She slapped his butt and said in her best imitation of the slang the Grays used, "well, thanks for that, honey, but Worship is a'startin' and we're a'gonna be late!" She ushered him down the hall to gather the kids so they could walk to the Worship center.

* * *

"And once the gentle folk were gathered up. Do you know what the Christians did?" The room was silent, hanging on the White's every word. "They shot them. With those horrendous, deadly, weapons of mass destruction. Assault rifles. Bullets tore through the innocents. The Christians butchered my ancestors. Those of my kind, who were born without the ability to cause harm. Born, by their very nature, to be the epitome of good. A model for all citizens. And a threat to the Christian teachings. For that, my kin were murdered. For their goodness they were killed. That night, those great men and women and children that we have gotten to know over the past few weeks, were slaughtered.

"You remember hearing of Angelina and her eight year old daughter Rashida. Angelina was killed. Rashida was spared the bullet, but not for her benefit. No, the Christian who 'saved' her took her alone and raped her. In front of Martina, her other mother. You remember when she was able to sneak her wife and daughter out from the basement they were hiding in? They were almost free when a Gray betrayed them. You see? Even some of those most trusted by us have turned on us in the past.

"Martina was shot, of course. But as she lay dying, the last thing she could see was her eight year old daughter being raped by a Christian. When the man was finished with her, he shot Rashida, too. All of the Whites gathered that night were killed. All. Not a single White lived through the burning of Atlanta." The White stopped talking, letting the uncomfortable silence fill the air.

Rhys felt his legs getting sore as he held the pose of worship. He was on his knees with his hands extended forward and his head touching the ground. It was a very uncomfortable pose, but he had gotten used to it over the years. Sometimes they were forced to hold this pose for hours while the White told stories from their history. Every night these lessons were taught. And every night, everyone in their district attended. Without fail. For hours, the Colors were stuck on their knees, offering worship to the Whites.

Rhys found worship boring. To keep his mind busy, he liked to remember his childhood. He had been born and grew up in a small town. When he was ten, he was taken from his parents. Or, his parents were taken from him, actually. He remembered some of the actual event, but not everything. He was told his parents had been Christian and part of a seditious group bent on spreading their hate filled doctrine.

Rhys actually remembered being taught of Christ as a child. He knew what the Whites taught was false. When he was a kid, he would gather with his family and several other families to study God's word. They called it 'life groups' and Rhys had been able to continue meeting in the Complex. It was like a home church. Life groups taught a lot about loving and serving everyone. Taught that everyone was equal and only one person was perfect, Jesus. Growing up, he learned that God truly loved everyone and wanted all people to love each other and follow His commands.

By the time he was ten, Rhys had memorized God's commandments along with several Bible verses. Rhys had been given his own Bible and enjoyed studying and reading it. He worked hard to make his mom and dad proud. His parents also taught him about the attacks of the enemy and warned him of the spiritual battle that was coming. Boy had they been right.

It was during a life group session that his parents were taken. He was told that his parents were evil and had been charged with hate speech. They were taken to be re-educated, but Rhys had never seen them again. He was taken to a large city and put in a commune with other 'victims' of Christianity. All children removed from a Christian home were raised together. They were re-educated and taught the true evils of Christianity: individual responsibility and the idea that there is only one God.

Rhys knew he would never see his parents, but decided early that he would honor them by continuing to follow God. However, he knew that he would have to hide it. To lay low and wait. He worked hard not to draw attention to himself as he was growing up. But he took every chance to live his life as if Christ were living his life. He treated others with kindness and love at every chance he got. And he had been blessed with a beautiful wife and two amazing children. How he had gotten so far without being caught was truly a miracle. Rhys trusted that God had a big plan for his life.

As the White finished her story, Rhys thought *if no one survived, how do they know what happened?* The White's voice began again, more softly now.

"It has been just over twenty five years since that night. And still Whites deal with the hatred and anger from Colors. Just today I was spit on by a Color while walking the street. After all we have done as your gods. We provide good, honest, meaningful work for the betterment of all mankind. We provide you with food. We provide you with housing. We provide you with knowledge. All this we do for free. All we ask in return is your worship and respect. That's all. Daily praise and adulation for a short time each night. For All Are One."

"And One Serves All," the room echoed back. The White stood in silence, looking over the group. She let the response echo off the walls of the small room. When the room was once again silent, she stepped away from the podium and began the long slow walk out of the worship center. The center of the building was an open, dirt

floor dug about a foot down into the middle. A raised platform surrounded the room, where several Grays stood. A small bridge led
through the sunken floor and to a circular island in the center of the
room with a podium at it. This is where the Whites stood every night
to preach. The sunken area was for the Colors to kneel and worship.
During the sermon, the Grays stood along the outer wall, bent to
one knee to listen. They were able to listen to the sermon and show
the Whites the proper respect while at the same time monitoring the
Colors for dissidence.

After about five minutes, the Grays left the building. The
Colors all maintained their pose of supplication. Finally, the bell rang
and the Colors stood. They divided into two lines and began a slow
march out of the building. As the passed through the door into the
night, Grays stood on either side. First, every Color was given the
Sacrament, a small tablet placed on their tongue. Then they moved
to the next gray and were given their food allotment.

Once through, Rhys and his family huddled together as they
walked. Rhys took everyone's food and Grace took all of their waters
so the children didn't have to carry it. As they moved further from
the Worship center they spit the tablets out, handing them to Rhys,
who quickly slid them into a pocket of his pants. They were careful
that none of the other Colors were watching as they did this. They
used the food and water transfers to mask what they did, but no one
really paid any attention to them. As he slid the pills into his pocket,
Rhys prayed thankfully to God that the Grays no longer patrolled
at night as his family walked home alone, lit only by the light of the
moon.

CHAPTER 10

The bell rang out, jolting Rhys awake. He sat up in bed and rubbed the sleep out of his eyes. He and Grace had been up late into the night, quietly talking about what she could do. They still hadn't come up with any new answers and went to sleep with the same plan they had when they started: to pray and trust God to deliver help. But, one thing they both knew for sure was that she was not going to help Connors.

If it came to it, they would try to run. Try to jump the fence and make it to the wilderness. What they would do from there, Rhys had no idea. He didn't know anything about providing for his family, but he thought Grace's work in the Gardens might come in handy. Rhys doubted he could even keep his family safe, though. The rebels from outside still attacked the compound regularly, killing a few Colors each time. Sometimes, a Gray would even be killed.

But, despite the risks, Rhys would rather take his chances than face the definite death at the order of Connors. Unfortunately, they really only had one chance to escape. The Whites were very severe in their punishment of deserters. Anyone caught attempting was declared a heathen Christian and crucified. Each worship hall had a small alcove with a single cross. The bodies were displayed as a reminder of what would happen to anyone selfish enough to abandon their brethren. Rhys shuddered in revulsion at the memory of the last man who tried to escape. It had been almost a year already but it felt like yesterday. He could still smell the man's body after a week on the cross. Rhys shook his head, trying to clear the thoughts away.

He and Grace had decided to trust God. If it was their time to go, well, *thy will be done.* If not, God would provide a way out. They just had to be alert and aware so they could watch for God's signs.

After the usual breakfast, morning conversation, and prayers, Rhys waved goodbye to his family. He watched as they walked toward the center of the Complex on their way to school and work. He turned and began his long walk toward the Gray's compound where his assignment would be posted. Rhys joined a group of other colorfully dressed, empty-eyed men. He tried to imitate the blank, uncaring stare of those around him.

Rhys remembered that feeling. When he stopped taking the Sacrament, his mind had cleared. He felt like himself again. He vowed never to take those pills again and stuck to it, for the most part. Once in a while he would have to swallow to avoid suspicion, but that didn't happen often. They Grays just didn't seem to care enough and were always in a hurry to go home after Worship. Rhys wasn't sure what they did at night, but they always seemed either groggy or angry in the mornings.

He rounded a corner and the Gray zone came into view. The entire complex was built in a large, circular shape. At the center of the circle was the White's Tower, surrounded by the Gray zone. This was an area open only to the Whites and Grays. The worship hall and the school were built along the line separating the Color districts and the Gray zone. Whites, Grays and Colors all made use of those buildings.

The Gray zone made up a rough, triangular shape surrounding the White's Tower. At the three points of the triangle, was the Gray compound. This was where the Grays ate, drank, and slept in a large communal setting. Each compound was in charge of three Color districts, which had been built in rows leading out to the outer wall. The outer wall was a large circle surrounding the entire Complex. Beyond that was a large, open, abandoned area. This was where the Rebels attacked from and where Rhys would be assigned if sent out scavenging.

Rhys knew he wouldn't be scavenging, but was curious what he'd be doing today. The Grays posted work groups each day on a large, black board on the side of compound. All Rhys had to look for was his symbol. This was tattooed on his arm so he wouldn't forget. He kept his head down as he moved closer, trying to get a view of the board. As he moved down the path, he noted several Grays posted and monitoring the group. These Grays looked almost as blank-eyed as the Colors, though.

Rhys had to look away as a Gray yawned, stretching his arm into the sky. None of the other Colors ever yawned back, but Rhys always felt himself wanting to yawn after seeing the Grays. It seemed like an easy way draw attention. He figured the Sacrament dulled the senses of the other Colors, so most of them wouldn't react. Once in a while, there would be a man who yawned back. Most people didn't seem to notice, but Rhys did. And so did a few of the Grays. The man Rhys had spoken to yesterday had been one of those he'd seen yawn in the past and that is part of why Rhys had been willing to open up to him even just a little bit.

Rhys followed the line of men as they approached the board. The men were very docile as they got their assignments. The Grays never had to tell them to line up, the men just formed themselves into a few lines, checking their assignments one-by-one. When the man in front of him stepped away, Rhys took his turn. He looked up at the large black board and quickly found his crew number.

Rhys was pleasantly surprised to see his crew was assigned to unload trucks today. He dropped his head and turned, immediately stepping away and moving toward the warehouse. He smiled as he walked, relieved that he'd be indoors. His neck and arms were still sore from the sunburn he'd gotten yesterday, and a day inside was a blessing. He prayed thanks to God as he moved through the district.

The warehouse was the only building that stood along the exterior wall. As Rhys approached, he had a brief view over the wall. Four trucks were lined up along the road. Rhys held out his left arm to the waiting Gray, displaying his marks. The Gray barely glanced down and nodded. Rhys bowed and then stepped through the door and into the shade of the building.

The air was warmer, but Rhys was relieved to be out of the sun. He walked across the open floor, and stood with the other waiting

Colors. When they had all arrived, the large door slid upward, letting in a gush of cool wind. Rhys closed his eyes, enjoying cool air. It was almost immediately replaced by a blast of warm air and the smell of the burning gas.

Rhys watched in awe as the first truck rolled forward. The power of the machine was astounding, and always left Rhys feeling impressed. He'd tried to tell Grace about the trucks once, but she didn't seem to understand it. She just shrugged and had said, "Guess I'd have to be there."

The truck stopped and the noise died. The back-end rolled up and a man jumped to the ground. He nodded to the gathered men and then walked out of the building. As he moved out of the way, he pulled a small, black box with a light on it from his pocket. Rhys's attention was drawn, as always, to the man's clothes. He was dressed very differently from anyone in the Complex. He wore tight fitting, clean pants and a button down shirt tucked into them. All of his clothing was clean and fit him very well. Rhys quickly surveyed those standing around him and saw all the men wearing torn, dirty, loose fitting clothing, patched together with a wild mix of colors. The Grays were the only ones who wore anything similar to the man's clothing, with their clean, military style uniforms. The Whites wore robes of pure white tailored only by Gray women and never touched by Colors.

"Attention," a Gray said loudly while stepping forward. The Colors bowed their heads and stood silently. "This truck is full of supplies for our Complex, sent to us from a neighboring city. It is to be unloaded from the truck and then transported to the designated locations in the warehouse. There it will be catalogued and then sorted for distribution throughout the Complex. Any questions?" The Colors remained silent. "Alright, then let's get to it!"

At that he clapped his hands and stepped away from the truck. Rhys stepped into the line that was forming behind the truck. Several other Colors stepped up into the truck. As they lined themselves up, Rhys saw one of the older men get pushed into the hardest spot on the line. Rhys couldn't take seeing the man suffer needlessly, so he moved out of his position and took the older man's spot.

As Rhys stepped between the man and the truck, the man offered Rhys a relieved smile. The man met Rhys's eyes, one of very few Colors willing to do that. Rhys could see a well of emotions in the man's eyes. Rhys quickly looked around to make sure he wasn't being watched. He felt a strong pull and followed his impulse. He showed the man a very quick sign of the cross.

The man looked shocked and then his face lit up with joy. He stepped forward as if to hug Rhys, but then stopped and looked around the room. No one was watching them, but the old man realized that they were surrounded by people who were watching for anything out of the ordinary. Guards who didn't want the men talking, let alone hugging. The man quickly turned back to face front, standing shoulder to shoulder with Rhys.

Rhys could feel excited energy radiating off the man's frame. He didn't recognize the man and realized he must be one of the new recruits that had been transported over from a neighboring city. Colors were assigned different cities from time to time depending on the needs and the number of Colors. Rhys felt lucky to have spent so much time in one city, even if things weren't great there. He at least felt comfort in the routine and he knew Grace really enjoyed working in the Garden. If they were moved to another city, she may not be assigned to the Gardens again. A loud sound pulled Rhys's attention back to his work. The Colors in the truck were in position and ready to start handing boxes down.

The first large, black, plastic box dropped to Rhys. He felt the weight smack painfully against his forearms. He passed it carefully to the older man and then stood ready for the next. Rinse and repeat. It was not easy work, but was pretty mindless. Once his arms went numb, Rhys actually enjoyed it. It gave him time to think. To pray. To recite what he knew of the Bible to himself in his mind. Wayne, Mary, and Charles were coming over for Church that night, and Rhys wanted to be prepared.

After a couple of hours, the first truck was emptied. The men all stepped back from their positions, allowing the Colors in the truck to jump out. Once it was all clear, the strange man climbed in the truck and backed it out of the warehouse. A second truck rolled forward and stopped in the same spot. This truck was full of water bottles, that just so happened to weigh more than the first boxes. Rhys felt his arms beginning to turn rubbery from the work, but knew there would be no stopping until all of the trucks were emptied.

After a full day unloading, Rhys was glad to finally hear, "Last box!" from above. He looked up just as the box sailed out above him. Rhys brought his arms up to catch it when his foot slipped. He felt his body swing off balance as the box hit him in the arms. His arms were pushed down by the weight of the box. His legs shot out behind him and he landed directly on the box. A large *crack* reverberated around the open walls of the warehouse.

The Grays rushed over to the truck, guns pointing at the noise. When they saw Rhys lying on the ground, they all burst out laughing. They laughed harder as Rhys worked frantically, trying to get his feet back under him. He almost fell again as he bent to pick up the box, but was able to stay on his feet. After a few seconds, which felt to him like hours, Rhys got his arms under and around the box. He put a lot of force into lifting it and was surprised at how light the box felt.

He was relieved to see the Grays moving away as he handed the box to the man next to him. "Clumsy-ass monkeys," he heard one Gray say. He dropped his head and felt his eyes shoot open. A shock of lightening ran down his spine as he stared at a small, white packet on the ground. He shot his foot forward, covering the packet with his boot, and slid it back under him. Rhys stood perfectly still, waiting to see if anyone had seen. He listened to the normal, bustling sounds of the room around him. He prayed no one had seen him.

The box was moving its way down the line and Rhys realized the Colors in the truck would be jumping out any second now. He had to get the packet or he'd be forced away. He glanced to the side and realized the older man was watching him. The older man nodded firmly. Rhys understood it to mean, "Go! Now!" and dropped quickly to the ground.

Rhys grabbed the packet and slid it into the inside of his sock. He shot back up and stood, holding perfectly still again. He felt the man nudge him in the arm but didn't hear anything out of the usual.

The man nudged him again and a loud voice rang out from above him saying, "You gonna move, man?"

Rhys jumped back as he realized the Color above him was trying to jump down. A Gray nearby looked their way, but then turned back to the room at large. Rhys could feel his heart racing as blood rushed through his neck. He realized he'd done it. He'd gotten whatever it was off the ground and could take it home. He prayed that Grace would know what to do with it now, but felt sure that God had just saved them.

CHAPTER 11

G race waved goodbye to Rhys and turned with the kids to start their day. Grace put her arms around her children's shoulders as they walked. They kept their heads down, trying not to look at each other. Grace shrunk away from the Gray guards that sporadically walked through the crowds. She thought of what Rhys had said about the Grays being posted high above everyone and felt herself shake, very glad that the women and children were guarded less severely.

They came to the mouth of the alley that led around the schoolhouse. Grace smiled at Lily, who was fiddling with her hair. Thomas just looked up at his mom, steeling himself as he prepared to say goodbye. His hands were bandaged from the day before and she knew he was afraid of it happening again. She saw the pain in his eyes but was proud of his courage. He was trying to be strong so she didn't worry. She felt a tear form in the corner of her eye.

She wanted to hug him but was able to hold herself back. Thomas was at an age where he didn't like to show affection like that. She suspected he didn't want to look weak. It had been hard, but she had decided to respect his desire to at least appear strong and courageous, even if he didn't fully feel it. "Gotta fake it to make it sometimes, hon," Rhys had said when they talked about it.

"I'll see you after school, mom," Thomas said quietly, smiling gently at her. He turned and started down the alley, fidgeting with the bandages on his hands. Grace smiled sadly to herself and then looked at Lily. She had become distracted with something. Grace followed her gaze and it landed on a young boy. The boy was staring back at Lily. Grace was happy to see the look of teenage love in their eyes, until she saw the Gray uniform the boy was wearing.

Grace turned back to her daughter and her stomach dropped. She was infatuated with this boy. Grace knew that look well, since she had worn it herself. Growing up, she had been a Gray, who fell for a Color. Her father had been a guard and her mother a Gardner, like her. Grace had to push away those memories, not wanting to get distracted.

"Lillian," Grace said quietly. "We need to talk." She pulled Lily into the alley, looking quickly around to make sure no one else was listening. The street had cleared for the moment and they were alone. Grace turned back to Lily and saw defiance in her eyes, and a hint of fear.

"Who is that boy?" Grace asked softly.

"Craig," Lily replied, simply. Grace was a little surprised that her daughter wasn't denying it.

"OK," Grace replied, thinking quickly. "OK, so you know it won't work, right?"

"Mom," Lily said, "Mom, I know. It's nothing. It's fun to fantasize about, but I know it wouldn't work. But you did get to be with dad, right? So it's not IMPOSSIBLE. Just very, very unlikely. Probably never will happen, though, and I know." Grace just watched Lily's face as she spoke. She read a broad mix of emotions, but Grace could read a subtle note of excitement in Lily's eyes.

Grace just stood for a moment, trying to process what her daughter had said. Grace was glad to hear Lily say it was nothing, but she couldn't quite bring herself to believe it. *But, maybe Lily is trying to convince herself, too,* Grace thought. She smiled at her daughter, shook her head, and pulled her in for a hug. They stood like that for a moment before separating.

"Lily, I love you. Just listen for a second, OK?" Grace said. Lily met her gaze and nodded. Grace continued, "You are a smart girl. I'm so impressed at how grown up you are. And I can see that you like this boy. I've been there. And you're right, there is a chance. It's very rare, but, if you are able to earn your robes, there is a chance."

Lily smiled at her mom, light filling her eyes. Grace couldn't bring herself to crush her daughter just yet. The chances of her earning even half what she'd need, were so slim as to be impossible. But Grace could never take that hope from her daughter. A life without hope is a very dark place. But she did need to bring her back to reality a little bit. She prayed that God would soften her daughter's heart.

"But," Grace said, "that being said, you're not going to get that chance if you get caught now, right?" Lily sobered up a little. She nodded at her mother, a serious look in her eyes as she listened to her mother's words. "Right. So, you need to be more careful than you are being right now. I can see you like him. I know he likes you. If I can see that in just a second, imagine what the Grays can see. You need to be smarter and not draw attention to yourselves until you are ready."

Grace was very glad to see that she had gotten through. She could see the earnestness in Lily's eyes as she stared back. "OK, mom," she said. "Thank you." Lily let out a sigh and then hugged her mom one more time. "I gotta go or I'm gonna be late."

"Yeah," Grace replied, "me too. Have a good day, hun. I love you so much."

"Love you too, mom," Lily replied, turning away. That serious look was still on her face. Grace could almost see the wheels turning in her daughter's brain.

"Lily," Grace said before Lily was out of earshot. Lily turned back and Grace continued, "I am very, very proud of you." Lily's smile widened and her cheeks brightened.

"Mom, stop," Lily said as she waved her hand. Grace smiled and watched as her beautiful, brave, intelligent daughter hustled down the dark, foul, grime covered alley toward school. She shook her head and continued toward the Gardens.

* * *

Grace was about halfway through her morning shift when the alarm sounded. All of the women immediately stopped what they were doing and crawled under their tables, putting their heads between their legs and their arms over their heads. Grace listened as the room cleared of Grays, all heading toward the wall to help with the defense. A small number of Grays remained, just enough to guard the women. Grace took a deep breath and settled in, trying to find a comfortable position.

It had been a few weeks since the last attack. Grace felt like they were becoming less frequent, but couldn't tell for sure. The alarm continued blaring through the room, echoing off the walls. Once comfortable, she distracted herself from the noise by repeating Bible verses in her head. She didn't know many, but enough to keep her mind busy. Rhys had always been better with memorization than she was, so he often took the lead in prayer and in recitation for the family.

She was just finishing Isaiah:53 for the second time, when the alarm stopped out, indicating an all clear. The women remained under their tables, waiting to be instructed to stand. The door opened and the Grays began filtering back into the room. When all were back in position, the officer Grace had seen yesterday strode toward the center of the room, stepping up to the small podium positioned there.

"Attention!" he called out loudly. The women all knew what to do immediately. This was the common way of providing any instructions or information. The women quickly and quietly walked toward the officer with their heads bowed. Once they arrived at their usual spot in front of the central podium, they dropped to their knees and assumed the position of worship. The room filled with a silent tension. Grace was just thinking maybe she should resume her Bible verses when the door opened.

Grace listened to a flurry of noise as several people rushed into the room. She wasn't sure what was happening but, after a few minutes, the noise stopped. The room waited expectantly again. Grace thought she could hear the soft padding of footsteps, but wasn't sure. Grace focused on her position, working hard not to fidget or show any signs of discomfort. She felt her muscles tensing as she strained to hold still.

From the podium in front of her, a soft, female voice said, "Our great city was once again besieged by Rebels today. Tragically, they were able to kill someone of importance today. Usually it is only the

Colors targeted by Rebels, but today was different. Today, one of our Grays gave his life in defense of this city." At her last words, the soft voice cracked. She stopped speaking for a moment and Grace heard her blow her nose.

When she began again, her voice was stronger, more firm, "The attack was on the northern wall. This serves as a great reminder of the importance of the work being done there. Without the orders of the Whites to provide for your protection, those savages may have gained entry and had access to our gentle people."

Grace could hear the emotions in the woman's voice. Hear the pride when speaking of the wall, the disgust when the Colors were mentioned, and the false sadness about the death of the Gray. Grace did all she could to suppress a shiver at her frustration with this woman. Ever since Rhys first introduced her to God and the Bible, she became more and more appalled at the Whites. She grew up, being told the Whites were gods living amongst men. She believed them to be superior to her in every way. Pure. Innocent. Righteous. Unable to cause harm. These things were drilled into her for as long as she could remember.

And not just that. She had been told that, once she became a Color, she was taking responsibility for the genocidal behavior of those that had come before her. Colors who had mindlessly slaughtered the innocent Whites during the Great Division. Once Grace began reading the Bible and learning of the message of Christ, she realized how wrong she had been. She still got chills when thinking about some of those early readings. The first time she read Romans 3:10, "There is none righteous, no, not one," she felt like she'd been electrocuted. Her spine tingled as a chill ran through her entire body and she felt her understanding shift. She felt for the first time what she realized later was the Holy Spirit, pulling at her attention.

It immediately reminded her of the lessons growing up. The Whites called themselves righteous quite often, but that was immediately disproved when you examined their behaviors. They ordered abuses, torture, and murder, as punishments for walking in the wrong spot. They had orgies together almost every night. They aborted the children conceived in these orgies as well. They were certainly not righteous. And Grace remembered thinking: *if they were lying about that, what else were they lying about?*

Grace pulled her attention back as the voice continued, "We have called in assistance from a local city. The death of so many has done some true emotional damage to many of the Whites here. The Whites are so sensitive that even such lowly deaths as those of Colors deeply affect us. The helicopter will arrive in fifteen minutes and the Whites wanted to give all a chance to prepare. You will maintain your positions of worship until the helicopter has departed. None of you are worthy of viewing the White who is coming, and you will not sully his view of our great city by exposing him to your faces. To the worst this city has to offer." The White stepped back from the podium.

"For All Are One," her voice echoed out.

"And One Serves All," the room echoed in response.

Grace kept her head down, listening as the room emptied. When it was silent again, she chanced a glance up. Standing in front of the Color women were two Grays. They slowly patrolled over the bowed heads of the Colors. Grace felt her chest relax at the realization that she was safe. She was uncomfortable but safe. She settled into her position and continued praying.

After a few minutes, a slow beating sound could be heard in the air. It grew louder and louder, eventually filling the room. A wind rushed through the open windows high along the walls of the Garden. Grace felt her head and shoulders physically lifted by the wind. She balanced on her knees and looked up in surprise. She met eyes with the Gray guard who seemed just as surprised as her. She almost smiled when she recognized it was Private Gates.

A piercing screech filled the air from above them. Grace looked up and felt her heart drop in terror as a big metal box broke off the ceiling. Her world dropped to slow motion as she tracked where the box would fall. She knew it was going to land directly on Private Gates.

Grace also knew she could save him. She didn't think. Grace leapt to her feet and raced toward the Gray.

He didn't seem to know how to react. Lucky for Grace he didn't raise his gun. He just stared in shock, not moving. Grace was grateful because it allowed her to plant her shoulder directly into his stomach. He doubled over and fell back with a grunt. Grace fell on top of him. As she was falling she heard two loud bangs, one right after another, followed by a ringing *PING* behind her.

Time stopped in Grace's mind as she tried to process what had all happened. A large metal box was lying behind her, right where Private Gates had been standing a moment before. Private Gates was now stuck under her, trying to catch his breath. He stared at her in shock. The other Gray was out of Grace's sight right now, but as she processed it, she realized the other bang had come from his gun. The *PING* must have been the bullet hitting the metal box then.

Time caught up with her again and she almost jumped off Private Gates. She stood and brushed herself off, trying not to think about how close she had come to getting crushed. Or shot. She put her hands up and stepped back, glancing over her shoulder to the other Gray. He nodded and put his gun down. Grace put her hands down and looked to Private Gates. He was just staring at her in shock and bewilderment. He looked about to say something, but Grace cut him off.

"I'm sorry, sir," she said quietly while bowing her head. She didn't wait for a response, but darted back to her spot and started praying again. She prayed nothing more would happen and was relieved when it didn't. The room was unusually silent for a short time, then the usual noise resumed as people fidgeted and the Grays walked slowly to patrol.

That was close, Grace thought. The more she thought about it, the more she felt God's hand in it all. That thought warmed her heart as she continued to pray, waiting until she could get back to work.

CHAPTER 12

G race walked into her home and was immediately attacked. Rhys swept her up into his arms and carried her to the kitchen, away from the window. Grace was able to keep herself from yelling out, but just barely.

"Don't do that," she said with a smile. She glanced back at the door, and relaxed at seeing the empty street. She looked back at Rhys's smiling face. When he didn't say anything, she said with a smile, "What's going on?"

"Guess what God delivered to me today," Rhys said quietly, with a small smile. Grace could see that he was barely holding back his excitement. She loved his enthusiasm and how he saw blessings from God in even the smallest things. She saw an opportunity to tease him and make him laugh.

"Oh my gosh," Grace replied. She put her hands over her mouth and said lightly, "Are you pregnant? Are we gonna be parents again?" She feigned delight and jumped up clapping her hands in front of her face silently.

"Har har," Rhys said sarcastically. Grace stopped and smiled. They held each other's gaze for a moment, Rhys waiting to make sure she was done before he continued, "No, it's this." He looked around the room once more then reached into his sock. He pulled out a small, white package with a picture of a cucumber on the front. Grace stared in shock at the small package, recognizing the seed packet, but at a complete loss for how Rhys would have gotten his hands on them. She had once seen a Color placed in the stocks for picking up a seed, never mind a packet. She knew personally that the

Grays kept a very strict inventory of all the seeds in the Gardens. And here Rhys was with a full, closed package.

She realized that it had been a long time and she hadn't said anything. She was just staring in shock at the packet, Rhys smiling in response. "How?" she asked. Rhys quickly told her the story and she sat down in disbelief, the seed packet in her hand. She wasn't sure what to do with them.

"Do you know what this means?" Rhys asked. Grace shook herself a little and looked to Rhys. "When you get those seeds from Connors, you can plant these instead! He'll never know and that will give us some time to figure out what to do without hurting anyone."

Grace ran through the scenario in her head for a second before realizing Rhys was obviously right. She pushed down the fear that bubbled up at the thought of lying to a White and was able to keep it at bay. Seeing the look of excitement in Rhys's eyes was very helpful in covering that fear. She closed her fist around the small packet and nodded to herself.

"We do need to hide this, though," she said. Rhys nodded and started looking around the room. Grace knew where they had to go, the only safe place. Unfortunately, getting to it was challenging. "We know where they have to go," she said. Rhys looked at her and then a resigned look crossed his face. He nodded.

"I'll hide it in here for now and we can put them away tonight," she said. "We have life group tonight anyways, plus Wayne said he's ready for his Bible, right? So we can get that out at the same time." Rhys nodded then pulled her in for a hug. After holding him for a minute, Grace said, "We better get cleaned up, don't want to be late." Rhys gave her a kiss and then left the room. Grace sat at the table, still holding the seed packet in her hand. She lifted the corner of the carpet and set them on the ground. She panicked at the idea of them being so exposed, but couldn't think of anything better. *Please let that be a good enough spot, God* she prayed.

* * *

"The pure and righteous protection, given by myself and the other Whites, was your salvation once again today." Rhys was on his knees, holding the pose of worship and listened to the gravelly male voice speaking at the podium. A different White spoke at their district's worship hall each night, ensuring all were worshipped equally. The man coughed, cleared his throat, and continued, "Were the Christians who attacked earlier able to get in, they would have killed as many of you as possible. Their hatred for you is more than even their hatred for us Whites. They see you as traitors and believe you should attack like they do. They want your anger. Your hatred.

"And, sadly, they would easily get it. You Colors remain a heathen lot. All we ask from you is worship. In return we ensure your safety, your security, your lives. But many of you resist. You are all one bad thought away from becoming those monsters. Your control on your darker selves remains tenuous because of your ties with your ancestors. The Whites are able to help, but it is up to each and every one of you to demonstrate your devotion.

"Have faith in us and we will continue to protect you. Continue to care for you, feed you, clothe you. We provide all. All you need do is bow and worship. And remember, those not worshipping may be dangerous. So please report any concerns to your Grays. Who knows, if your concerns are found to be valid, you, any of you, may earn your Gray robes."

The room was held in silence for a moment. "For All Are One," the White said.

"And One Serves All," the crowd repeated.

Rhys and Grace walked a little more quickly getting home that night. Their Bible meetings with Wayne and Mary were the highlight of their week, but they were only able to get together at night after the Grays had left. Rhys suspected the streets weren't patrolled at night only because of the Sacrament that was given to the Colors after worship. He remembered the euphoric feeling they gave, but along with that came a grogginess and then within about an hour silent, undreaming sleep. The following morning, his mind was foggy and his thoughts were slow. All of that had stopped as soon as he'd stopped taking the pills. His family and Wayne and Mary had experienced the same thing.

They got home and immediately lit the candle on the table and stoked the fire in the hearth. They ate quickly by candle light, being sure to leave enough food for breakfast the next morning. Rhys wanted everything to be cleaned up before Wayne arrived, so he was rushing his family a little. After supper Rhys and Grace worked together to hide the seeds. Rhys first stuck his head out the window and looked up and down the street. All of the windows he could see were dark and there wasn't a soul in sight. Satisfied they were safe, he stepped back into the kitchen to join Grace. She was holding the packet of seeds in her hand.

One of the first things they'd done when they moved into the shack was dig out a large hole in the center of their kitchen to hide their Bible. Over the past few years, Rhys had collected a number of other things that were stored there as well. Rhys wanted a distraction, things bad enough to hide but he prayed not enough to get them killed. Pictures and books and some small statues. Things of beauty and creativity that reminded Rhys and his family of God in a way. Or at least that man had been made in God's image.

Those less severe items were hidden in a small hole Rhys dug under the kitchen table. Rhys and Grace worked together to first move the table and then the carpet, being careful to stay out of sight of the window. The street was silent but better safe than sorry. They looked down into the small pit and admired the things they'd collected. Grace smiled at each item as Rhys handed them to her. They had an old photobooks with pictures of an openly Christian family. There was a journal from before the Division and a few books, each written by Christians.

Grace had a small pile next to her when the pit was emptied. Now all they were able to see was a dark plastic sheet. Rhys pulled that sheet out, exposing a square of dirt. Then, he reached in with both arms, grabbing small metal handles on the outside edges. He lifted a metal tray covered with dirt and carefully pulled it out, setting it aside. Now Rhys could see the true treasure, three Bibles. He pulled two out quickly as Grace put the small pack of seeds in. Then they replaced everything in reverse order: metal tray, plastic, and memorabilia. When it was all back, they put the rug and table back and stood to double check their work. They left the Bible on the seat of a chair pushed into the table.

A short time later, a muffled knock came from the door. It followed the usual rhythm, tap, tap-tap, tap. Rhys rushed to the living room and opened the door, letting in a small family. Wayne was about the same age as Rhys. They had met on work duty and known each other longer than they'd known their wives. Wayne was fairly new and overheard Rhys say "gosh" when he hammered his thumb at work. Rhys had a deeply ingrained habit of not taking the Lord's name in vain, but his use of "gosh" made him stand out. He tried hard not to use the term, but it slipped that day, one of very few instances. And that happened to be the time Wayne overheard. God's intervention.

Over the course of the next three months, the men chatted when possible and arranged to meet for weekly Bible studies they called Life Groups. Both men were desperate to speak openly with another believer. Rhys told Wayne to spit out the Sacrament, and they had their nights free. They still only met once a week, not wanting to expose themselves too much, but it was enough. They'd been meeting one night every week ever since, taking turns hosting. As their families grew, their Life Group grew as well.

The past few weeks, Wayne and Rhys had been discussing getting Wayne's son Charles his own copy of the Bible. Tonight was the night. Charles had just turned fourteen, and Wayne felt he was ready to take ownership of his faith. Wayne knew that Rhys had a couple of extra Bibles. Not only that, but Rhys hated hiding the Bible away. It felt like something that needed to be shared, needed to be spread. Bibles were made to be in the hands of believers, blessing lives and spreading love, not buried under his table.

Rhys smiled as we welcomed in his friends. They felt like a true family at Life Group. Thomas greeted Charles at the door, guiding him energetically down the hall into his room. Apparently he had made up a new game and was very eager to show it off. Thomas loved having Charles over and was always ready with something new to show off. They liked to wrestle too, which Rhys encouraged so long as they weren't so loud they would draw attention.

This gave Rhys and Grace privacy and lots of time to talk with Wayne and Mary. They had all become very fast friends and confidantes. They spoke often of the Bible, doing studies and breaking down God's word. But they also talked about their daily lives, each helping the other carry their burdens. Just having another family to talk to openly was such a relief it was worth any danger.

Rhys led Wayne and Mary into the kitchen and asked Lily to get the boys. When they were all together Rhys said, "Tonight is a special night. I have something for you, Wayne." With that, Rhys picked up the Bible off the table.

Wayne and Mary's faces immediately became serious. "You really think he's ready for it?" Wayne asked. Rhys could read a slight look of fear on Wayne's face, but it was overshadowed by a look of excitement and eagerness with a hint of pride.

"You tell me," Rhys replied. "Is he ready for it?" Wayne looked to Mary, then pulled Charles into himself and nodded. "Alright then," Rhys continued, "There's only one thing left to do." Rhys stepped to the kitchen and pulled up a bucket of water that had been boiled and purified. Mary was initially confused, but seemed to understand pretty quickly.

Rhys met each of their eyes, starting with Wayne, moving onto Mary, and ending with Charles as he spoke, saying, "We hear our Lord and savior, Jesus Christ say in Matthew 28: 'all authority has been given to Me. Go therefore and make disciples of all nations, baptizing them in the name of the Father, and of the Son, and of the Holy Spirit, and teaching them to obey everything that I have commanded you. And remember, I am always with you, to the end of the age.'"

Rhys smiled as he noticed a tear building up in the corner of Mary's eye as she looked proudly at her son. She brushed it away as Rhys continued. "Baptism is a sign and seal of God's promises to this covenant people. In baptism God promises by grace alone: to forgive our sins; to adopt us into the Body of Christ, the Church; to send the Holy Spirit daily to renew and cleanse us; and to resurrect us to eternal life. Through Baptism, Christ calls us to new obedience: to love and trust God completely; to forsake the evil of the world; and to live a new and holy life.

"Through Baptism, we all become one Church, one body with Christ. Do you, Charles, accept God's grace and the salvation through Jesus and will you all work to live on mission and spread the love and joy of Christ throughout this fallen world?"

Charles had a very intent look on his face. Rhys was impressed at how seriously he was taking the Baptism. He answered solemnly, "I do and I will, with God's help."

"And part of that covenant is support from fellow believers, so," Rhys looked at each in turn as he said, "Wayne, Mary, Grace, Lily, Thomas, will you work with the gifts given you by God to support, encourage, and strengthen this family?"

"We will, with God's help," the group replied.

Rhys reached into the bucket, wetting his hand. He placed the sign of the cross on his forehead as he said, "Charles, I baptize you in the name of the Father, and of the Son, and of the Holy Spirit. May the Lord bless you and keep you; may the Lord cause His face to shine upon you and be gracious to you; and may the Lord lift His countenance upon you, and grant you peace. Amen."

Rhys held out the Bible to Wayne. Wayne took the Bible, then turned to hand it to Charles. As he took the Bible, Rhys said, "Charles, we grant you this Bible for your own studies. Guard and protect it, but study it and learn the words God sent to us. Share that word with your family that you may all know God's will and God's plan for your lives."

Charles took the Bible and then shook Rhys's outstretched hand. He met Rhys's gaze and nodded, then met the smiling face of Wayne. The held that look for a moment before Wayne pulled Charles into a tight hug. Mary joined in as well and the family stood in silence.

A few seconds later, Thomas asked, "Dad, can we go play now?"

The room broke out in quiet laughter as the hug broke apart chuckling. Before Charles could leave, Rhys said, "Remember, Charles. This is important and this makes you special. God loves you and wants you to spread His blessings to all those around you." Charles nodded and followed Thomas down the hall.

Mary's eyes were filled with tears as she watched Charles leave the room. She turned and hugged her husband again then took her seat at the table. Rhys joined them, setting the Bible near the candle at the center of the table. When they were all sitting, he used the ribbon to open the book. Once he found the spot they left off, he looked up to make sure they were all ready. He smiled at the joy evident on Wayne and Mary's face. Then he met his wife's loving gaze as he cleared his throat and looked down.

"John:15" Rhys read the whole chapter out loud, though quietly enough that his voice wouldn't carry:

"I am the vine; you are the branches,"

"As the Father has loved me, so have I loved you. Now remain in My love."

"If the world hates you, keep in mind that it hated Me first."

"When the Advocate comes, whom I will send to you from the Father—the Spirit of truth who goes out from the Father—He will testify about Me. And you also must testify,"

"Wow," Wayne said when Rhys was finished. "How does Jesus always find the perfect words? Probably helps to be the Son of God, I suppose." He smiled at his wife. They continued talking well into the night. This was how their studies usually went. They would read an entire chapter and then discuss it. They kept the Bible open for reference but talked to each other about how the passage spoke to them, or what they resonated with that week. Their conversations varied throughout the night from light hearted and fun, to angry, to helpless and everything in between. The only rule was to be open and treat each other with love. Honesty was always the best and they didn't hide their emotions. If they were mad, they showed it. And then the rest of the group would help show where God was trying to get their attention.

Rhys looked around the table as they talked, amazed at how blessed he was. Blessed to have a beautiful wife and family, good friends, a safe house, and enough to eat. The fact that they hadn't been taken yet was nothing short of miraculous. It could happen at any time that there would be a raid during their Life Group session, in which case they would all be caught and killed. *The Lord gives and the Lord takes away,* Rhys thought to himself. As always, it reminded him to appreciate the good he had in the moment, because it could be gone at any time. He smiled and basked in the company of friends. True, honest friends.

CHAPTER 13

R hys was sitting at his kitchen table, reading his Bible by candle light when he heard Grace call out from their bedroom. He
grabbed the candle and rushed out of the kitchen, careful to avoid
the clutter around the open pit in the center of the room. He left it
open while he was reading his Bible so he could quickly return it to
its hiding place if he heard a raid starting. As he came to his bedroom, he found Grace lying on the floor next to her bed. She had a
panicked look on her face and was trying to catch her breath with her
hand on her chest. Rhys set the candle on the floor next to her and
dropped to her side.

"Another dream, hun?" he asked quietly. Grace only nodded,
unable to speak right now. She was looking around the room trying
to get her bearings. Rhys sat next to her and started praying. He put
his arm around her and pulled her head against his chest, running
his fingers through her hair. He whispered one of her favorite verses
while he felt her sway against him.

"The Lord is my shepherd; I shall not want. He makes me lie
down in green pastures. He leads me beside still waters. He restores
my soul. He leads me in paths of righteousness for His name's sake.
Even though I walk through the valley of the shadow of death, I
will fear no evil, for You are with me; Your rod and Your staff, they
comfort me."

He recited this three times, whispering slowly and softly while
pressing his cheek against Grace's head. After the first, she had
calmed. She rocked gently in his arms while listening to the second
and then climbed back under the thin, ragged blanket. By the end of

the third time through, she was back asleep. Rhys smiled to himself as he looked at the peaceful, sleeping face of his beautiful wife. He was truly a blessed man.

As he slowly left the room, he thought about the past three weeks and the strain it had put on his wife. She was a very gentle soul and he loved her dearly for it, but she was not handling this stress well. She had been jumping at every sudden noise, and he had to remind her not to stare at their hidden compartment. She was often distracted during meals, too so he couldn't imagine how work was going for her. The anticipation seemed to be literally killing her and they couldn't figure out what Connors was waiting for. Rhys had actually suggested that Grace swallow the nightly Sacrament to maybe take the edge off. She hadn't even wanted to hear it and immediately rejected the idea.

Luckily, their "jobs" were as mindless as possible. Rhys realized she was probably less likely to stand out if she was worrying about getting caught than if she was as confident as she had been before all this started. Most of the women that Rhys saw wore either blank, empty faces, or were skittish and quiet. Very few, if any, met his gaze. That was pretty consistent behavior throughout all of the Colors, though.

His kids had been raised to mimic the behavior of the other Colors they saw. He had noticed his children, along with Charles, held themselves differently. They were much more likely to smile at others. Much more open to meeting your gaze. Rhys didn't want them to draw any extra attention to themselves, so he had taught his kids to keep their heads down throughout the day. *I'll have to remind Wayne to teach Charles that as well,* Rhys thought to himself as he sat back at the chair in the kitchen.

He put the candle on the table, and continued reading God's word. He tried to get his Bible out as often as he could, but he did have to be careful how he used his candles. They weren't easy or cheap to get, each candle costing a full credit. Grace could get needles and enough thread for five sets of clothing for that. But they both knew the extra light was essential. Rhys just had to budget his candle use to make sure they had enough light to get through until the next market day. Market day was the following day so Rhys could use as much of his candle tonight as he wanted.

Every six days, Rhys's work crew was allowed to shop at the market before worship, using any credits they had earned to purchase some luxury items. Things like fabric, dishes/silverware, firewood, spices, and candles. This allowed the Grays to manage the inventory and ensure each Color had access to the same things and none were given special treatment. Unfortunately, market day also meant that Rhys would be assigned salvage the next morning.

Rhys finished the chapter he was studying and closed the Bible. He put everything back in the hidden compartment under the table before shifting the table back over the rug. He stoked the fire once more, putting in enough wood to ensure it would stay warm through-out the night. Then he stirred the contents of the pot hanging over the fire before going to bed.

* * *

Rhys tried not to acknowledge the Gray guard peeking into the home, but instead focused on his work. He was in an abandoned, dilapidated house, pulling walls apart to gather wood. He would pull the drywall off and then use a saw and crowbar to remove the wooden supports holding the house up. The Gray, satisfied with whatever he saw, nodded and then continued his patrol. The build-ings were known to collapse periodically, so most Grays tried to stay far enough away to not be in danger, but close enough to keep an eye on the Colors.

Like all the Color jobs, it was hard work, but pretty mindless. If any Gray thought Rhys wasn't working hard enough, he would be punished. Whips were used pretty regularly and the work continued at an even pace. The Colors kept each other in line as well, ensuring none of their own were working too hard. That would make the rest look bad and would increase the work expected from them. What was achieved was work performed at a slow but very steady pace.

Rhys had been assigned demolition, meaning he was in the room, tearing out the nails and removing the walls. His partner,

Samuel, the old man he'd helped at the truck, was the runner. Samuel took the boards from Rhys and carried them to a large wagon, where they were stacked by another set of Colors. Rhys liked being inside, but it was definitely the more dangerous job. He had to be careful removing wood that wouldn't make the entire building collapse. So long as they were able to get enough wood out of the house, it would be left standing. The only problem was that the Grays decided when enough wood was removed. The Colors worked until they were told to move on to a new house. Rhys cut the last board off the wall he felt comfortable taking and handed it back to Samuel.

Ever since their moment at the truck, Samuel had been working near Rhys whenever possible. Rhys was assigned three separate work groups, all tattooed on his arm. Group 6, group C, and group Δ. Samuel was part of group Δ, one of his smaller groups. About the only time Rhys worked with him was on his weekly salvage jobs and the occasional bonus job they were assigned. Rhys wished they were able to work together more. He found comfort in the man's presence. Rhys had invited Samuel to join his Life Group, but Samuel wasn't comfortable sneaking out.

Rhys met Samuel's gaze as he returned to from the wagon. He smiled and said, "I'm gonna go into the next room, keep an eye on the roof for me?" Samuel nodded back solemnly. Rhys felt reassured and turned back to the room. He stepped through the hole he had just gutted into the wall and surveyed the next room. The light shone through a window on his left. He could see specks of dust floating in the air, dancing in the light beam. He stepped carefully around the pile of broken furniture in the center of the room.

Before the Colors could salvage, Grays swept through the buildings and removed anything that might be dangerous. Knives, weapons, books, pictures, anything deemed by the Whites as inappropriate for the Colors to see. The rest was piled in the center of the room and forgotten. These piles are where Rhys had found his small, hidden collection.

Rhys looked up the wall and followed the frame of the roof. He picked a wall leading from the center of the house toward the outside, not along the center and used his crowbar to break a few small holes in the wall. He wasn't sure if he was right or not, but he always tried to break these walls and avoided walls running along the center. So far, he hadn't been crushed. He glanced into the space behind the wall, finding the studs.

Once he'd located where the boards were, he used his crowbar to carve out a straight line in the dry wall. Once he'd cut a large enough section, he grabbed and pulled, breaking it off from the rest of the wall. He threw this scrap into the pile in the middle of the room. His heart froze as he looked back to the wall.

Lying on the floor in front of him was a Bible. It must have been hidden behind the wall he had just removed. It was obviously old but still in good condition. Rhys quickly double checked to make sure he was alone. He could see Samuel but no Grays were in sight. They patrolled the small area the Colors worked. Rhys quickly calculated how much time had passed since the last Gray had checked on him and realized they were due for another check any minute now.

Rhys got Samuel's attention and pointed to his eyes. They had found a chance to speak and had established this as a way to say: *Watch out for me.* The few times they had been able to use the signal, it had been very helpful. Samuel nodded back and glanced around what he could see outside of the building. Once he knew the coast was clear, Samuel nodded back a Rhys.

Rhys jumped into action, moving forward quickly and grabbing the Bible. He untied his loose fitting pants and pulled them out, allowing him to access the hidden pocket Grace had sewn into his pants. Somehow, Grace had found an elastic band and had put in around the center of the pocket, keeping whatever he might be able to grab close to his leg and in place. Rhys smiled at his wife's ingenuity as he slid the Bible down his leg and into the pocket, feeling the weight of it press against his inner thigh.

Rhys stood quickly and retied his pants. Then he glanced over his shoulder at Samuel, giving him another nod that he was finished. Rhys turned back to the wall and broke another section out. As he continued working, it was all he could do to actively stop himself from touching the book. He prayed for calm and strength, trying hard not to act unusual. He could feel the tension in his body, but must have been doing a decent job hiding it. Several Grays checked on them and moved on without comment. Rhys was just handing a board to Samuel when the shooting started.

CHAPTER 14

Rhys and Samuel immediately fell to the ground as the sound of gunfire rang out over them. They dropped the board and Rhys grabbed Samuel's arms, pulling him into the building. He heard bullets tearing through the wall above their heads. He put his back to what was left of the wall, trying his best to stay out of sight. Samuel was sitting against the wall next to him, holding his chest and trying to catch his breath.

Rhys peeked out from around the corner, looking out into the street to try to figure out what was going on. He saw the Grays fleeing, pointing their guns over their shoulders and spraying bullets randomly down the street. Rhys ducked again quickly as a bullet hit the wall near him. *Idiots,* he thought to himself.

The shooting stopped for a second, so Rhys looked out again. He knew it wasn't safe for him and Samuel to stay there. The Rebels had to be attacking and they were not known for taking prisoners. He just wasn't sure what direction they were coming from. The Grays seemed to be running down the street, back toward the Complex, but the Rebels often attacked from the trees. There was a small forest across the road from the building they were demolishing.

Rhys watched the trees, looking for any indication of people moving there. He didn't see anything, but he did hear distant shouts, followed by single gunshots. Loud voices were moving closer to him and Samuel. Rhys pulled his head back in and turned to Samuel. "The trees seem clear, I think they're our only option," Rhys said quietly.

Samuel leaned over Rhys, looking through the hole in the wall. He took in the distance and then nodded saying, "I think I can make it. Don't wait for me though. You get to those trees quick as you can." Rhys nodded in agreement but just to get them moving. He knew he could never leave the man behind. They both turned and crouched at the hole, wanting to find cover as soon as possible.

They looked out into the open street, followed by a short field and then the trees. They heard the voices getting closer and Rhys held up three fingers, counting them down. Rhys prayed hard for safety and protection as he counted. As his last finger dropped, Rhys pushed forward, out of shelter and onto the street. He didn't look to the side at all, keeping his eyes forward. He kept a hand firmly under Samuel's arm, making sure that the older man kept up.

No shots rang out. No voices started yelling at them. Within seconds, they were in the trees and stopped moving. Rhys caught his breath for a moment before looking back toward the house. He didn't see any movement and breathed a sigh of relief at realizing they'd made it. Feeling more secure in his position, he looked up the street to the Rebels.

He could just make out a small group of five men in the distance. Rhys was shocked he and Samuel hadn't been seen and prayed his gratitude to God. The men walked down the street, stopping at each house to go inside. Rhys thought about turning away when one man returned the street, pulling a Color out by her hair. He watched in horror as a second man pulled out a small handgun and shot her in the head. Her body dropped and Rhys realized he could make out several more clumps on the road behind the Rebels.

He felt himself filling with anger at the callousness of the men he was watching. They were chatting and laughing amongst themselves as they killed his fellow Colors. Rhys didn't know many of those killed personally, but recognized them all. As he watched, a group of Grays rounded the corner and started moving toward the Rebels. For the first time, Rhys was relieved to be seeing his guards.

They moved forward, guns out, closing on the Rebels. Rhys was confused as to why the Grays weren't shooting at all. The Rebels saw them coming and put up their hands. Then they waved. They smiled and waved at the Grays before turning and leaving. Rhys couldn't make sense of it but was glad to see them going. They Grays followed the Rebels, making sure they left the area and didn't continue their attack, Rhys assumed.

Rhys stood in the trees, waiting. He finally turned back and made eye contact with Samuel. Samuel had been watching with Rhys and seemed just as baffled as him. They could only stare, each at a loss for words. Rhys jumped and almost yelled out as a black figure stepped out from behind a tree near them.

"I mean no harm," the man said quickly and quietly. His hands were raised on either side of him and he spoke in a very gentle voice. "I bring only blessings from Jesus."

Rhys was just about to run back, but stopped at hearing the man say God's name. Rhys looked more closely at the man, wondering if he could be trusted. The man stood quietly, hands held up in front of him. He was clothed head to toe in black robes. Around his neck, he wore a cross on a necklace. Rhys had to keep himself from grabbing it and telling the man to hide it.

"Well then what *do* you mean," Rhys asked after a minute. The man had seen Rhys acknowledge his cross and smiled at him.

"I've seen you. I saw what you did with the deer a few weeks ago. I also saw you pray over the poor thing's body. You seem like a good man whom God sent to me for help. You know what this is?" the man asked, holding up his cross.

"I do," Rhys replied simply. He wasn't sure what the man wanted but was not about to reveal himself as believer to a stranger. Rhys was surprised to hear he'd been watched, but thought about their location. He realized they were fairly close to where he'd seen the deer and that the trees they were in now must be a part of the same forest.

"Good," the man smiled. He kissed the cross and then let it go, to hang around his neck again. An open display that would get him killed in a second in the complex. Rhys wasn't sure what to make of it, but listened carefully as the man continued speaking. "I mean to offer help. I know what life is like in there. I want to help you get out. I want to provide you a way to safety. To no longer live in fear. A way to a better life."

Rhys and Samuel just stared at the man, neither speaking. Eventually, Rhys said, "Who are you?" He wasn't sure what else to say. It sounded too good to be true and he didn't know if he could trust this man. "Are you a Rebel?" Rhys asked quickly, stepping back.

They heard constant horror stories about the terrors committed by the Rebels. Reports came in at least monthly of Rebel attacks and Colors were always being hurt or killed. Rhys tried to match what he'd been told about Rebels with the man standing before him. They didn't fit, so this man must not be a Rebel.

"I am what you have been told is a Rebel, yes," the man said simply. Rhys was surprised at his openness and honesty. He looked to Samuel unsure of what to say.

After a moment, Rhys replied with all he could think of, which was, "Well then why haven't you killed us yet?"

The man let out a sad sigh before saying, "We aren't the monsters you have been told about. Trust me. I do not want to harm you. I have no weapon. God knows I fail at it, but I try not to hurt anyone. Ever. You have been taught a lie."

Rhys stood mute, unsure if he should believe this man or not. He couldn't think of anything the man would get from lying to him, but he couldn't just bring himself to believe him either. He was taught a lie? About what? The Rebels? That was taught all the time. Every night. By the Whites. The more he thought about it, the more it made sense. He found himself believing. Rhys realized no one had said anything for quite a while.

Suddenly, they heard voices laughing. They looked up the street at the Grays who were returning. Rhys and Samuel met each other's eyes. Rhys realized that Samuel believed the man too. The strange man glanced at the Grays and whispered, "I have to go. Come with me and I will protect you."

Samuel almost immediately stepped toward the man, but Rhys couldn't. He knew he couldn't leave his family. He shook his head and said, "My family's in there. I can't."

The man started talking quickly. "Good. I'm glad to hear that. We want to save them too. We want to help you all. And any you can take out with you. Do you know a place in your complex called the Bronze gate?" Rhys nodded. "Good," Samuel continued. "At 1:00 AM every Sunday night, the guard there leaves his post for 15 minutes. If you can get your family there on Sunday night, one of my people will meet you outside the gate. From there, you will be escorted to safety."

Rhys's head was reeling with the new information. "What is 1:00 AM?" Rhys asked.

"That's right," the man replied, "no clocks. Close one. Alright well it'll be hard to tell exactly but go a few hours after dark. Find a place to hide and wait. The guard will give a sign that he's leaving his post, so you'll know when it's time. Go to that address in three nights after dark and wait. That's the best I can say. I will pray for you." The man glanced around the trees and back to the street. The Grays had passed the house Rhys and Samuel had been working at and were starting to yell to the Colors to get back to work. Rhys knew he needed to go soon or he'd be whipped.

"Wait, what if I can't make it?" Rhys asked. It was all happening so fast he didn't know if he would be able to arrange it.

"If you can't make it this week, we have someone there every week. Every seven days in the middle of the night, the guard will leave his post for a time, allowing any we are able to reach a chance to escape. If you don't make it this week, try again the following week, and the next after that until you can get out. We will be waiting." Rhys nodded and then stepped to Samuel, holding out his arms. Samuel smiled and stepped into the hug.

"I'll see you again soon, Rhys," Samuel sounded like he was about to cry. "And thanks for the help, brother. Take care of that family and come join us." Rhys could only nod as Samuel turned and followed the man deeper into the woods. When they were out of sight, Rhys started walking back to the complex. Rhys wiped a tear away from his eyes as he stepped out of the trees and into the sunlight. Rhys held his hands over his head and kept his head bowed.

Rhys didn't have to try very hard to look skittish and scared. He felt all of that and more. The Grays saw him and pointed their guns at him. When they realized he was a Color, the dropped their weapons and yelled at him to get back to work, motioning with their guns. Rhys returned to his building and resumed tearing out the walls. It was a little harder without Samuel there, but Rhys settled into a comfortable rhythm. He was much slower though and found his mind wandering. He thought of the strange man, of Samuel, wondering what Samuel was doing, thought of his first time meeting Samuel and of the excitement on Samuel's face as they said goodbye.

"Hey," a voice called out, bringing Rhys back into the moment, "you just gonna stand there and smile or you gonna toss me that board?"

Rhys was surprised to see the man he had spoken with a few weeks ago while building the wall standing outside the house. He had taken Samuel's place and was waiting for Rhys to hand him a board. The man was shaking his head at Rhys but he didn't look angry. More confused. They worked together in silence for a few minutes, before the man spoke again.

"Why you always smilin' man?" The man was speaking quietly, glancing over his shoulder, watching out for the Grays. Rhys realized that they had a moment alone. There weren't any Grays in sight. Rhys glanced down the street and saw the Grays huddled together, chatting and smiling, motioning back toward where the "Rebels" had gone.

"You really want to know?" Rhys asked. He motioned the man into the building. The man looked over his shoulder one last time and then followed Rhys into the building. When they had a moment of privacy, Rhys said, "I smile because I've been saved. I've got Jesus." Rhys was worried about this man's response, but felt himself compelled to talk. He'd learnt to trust these intuitions and felt them to be whispers from the Holy Spirit encouraging him to spread God's word.

The man gave him a questioning look. "Jesus," he said simply. Rhys could hear the disbelief in the man's voice. A moment of silence filled the air and Rhys waited anxiously. The man could turn him in to the Grays and that would be it. Rhys would be killed for blasphemy. "That's it? That's your secret? A made up guy in the sky?"

Rhys smiled and shook his head, relieved at the man's tone. He knew the man didn't believe him, but also knew the man wasn't going to report him. All Rhys could do was nod, smile, and shrug his shoulders. He met the man's gaze intently. When neither of them said anything the man continued, "I don't know, man. I know I'm s'posed to tell them about you but I won't. I just don't get how you get anything outta that."

Rhys felt his heart lighten at the man's words. It was pretty rare, but he'd been in this situation before. He knew the man would be open to hearing at least some of the truth. Rhys started, "Well, its not about me. I follow because it is the truth. Because there is one God who loves me so much He sent His only Son to die that I might have eternal life."

"Well, OK, but if your God loved you so much, how come you're here? How come you suffer in this place every day? How come those people out there are dead right now?" The man wasn't angry, but was obviously upset and hurting.

Rhys looked at him solemnly and replied, "I don't know." The man was surprised but before he could start talking, Rhys continued. "I'm sorry, but I don't have those answers. I don't know the exact, specific reason for all of the suffering, but I know that I trust God. I trust that He has a reason. I trust that I am here for a purpose and that my suffering will mean something."

Rhys spoke with as much sincerity as he could muster, which wasn't difficult because he truly believed what he was saying. He had practiced this a few times, but he worked to be as genuine as he could and let the Holy Spirit guide his words. The other man was paying rapt attention and didn't seem to want Rhys to stop, so he didn't.

"God is all good and I know He loves me. How do I know? Because He sent his Son to die for me. Any suffering I am facing now, is nothing compared to the suffering Jesus went through for me at the cross. If He can do that, I can bear this. And I trust that by bearing this well and following Jesus as closely as I can, God will turn this suffering into something good."

"Wow," the man replied. He shook his head and seemed to come back to himself. He looked around and Rhys could see the fear returning to the man's face. The man turned back to Rhys and said, "I don't know man. Don't tell no one this, but I tried it. I prayed so hard that God would just get me out, and He didn't listen. He ignored me. Now, how can He let me go through this after I asked Him to help?"

Rhys listened, shocked at the man's confession. After a moment of thought, Rhys said, "Well that's just it, you weren't asking for *God's will* to be done, but *yours*. You were testing God, saying, answer my prayers or I won't believe. You didn't really trust Him. Didn't really think He'd get you out. You weren't willing to follow Him until after you'd seen His power. It's like you were trying to make God prove He was worthy of you when it should ALWAYS be the other way around."

The man was initially stunned at Rhys's words but his face quickly turned to annoyance. Before he could reply, Rhys continued, "Yes. I do think you are deserving of this life. As am I. And I'm worthy of a hell of a lot more in the next life. Only through Christ am I saved. Nothing I do can ever, will ever, be enough to earn God's presence. He came to rescue me when I did nothing to earn it. I can't earn it. And neither can you. If God had wanted to answer your prayers, He would have. He has a reason for you to be here."

"It's up to you to find that reason and make it something for God's glory," Rhys finished quickly. He heard the Grays approaching again. "In the meantime, you may want to accept Christ's sacrifice in your heart and truly repent for your sins. You need to be begging for forgiveness from Christ." The man was about to speak, but Rhys cut him off. "No. Go now and put this board on the wagon. The Grays are coming." The man's eyes shot open.

He looked through the door and then back to Rhys. Rhys put the board in the man's arms and pushed him toward the opening. The man quickly composed himself and started moving to the wagon, head down. The Gray outside the house slowly walked past, gun out, surveying all the Colors. Rhys was careful not to draw attention to himself as he turned his head back to his work.

What a day, Rhys thought to himself.

CHAPTER 15

"**B**ut how do you know we can trust him?" Mary asked across the table.

"I don't know," Lily heard Rhys reply. Lily could hear the exhaustion in his voice. Her parents had told her some of what they've been going through but not enough for her to fully understand. They were together for Life Group with Wayne and Mary. Lily was thrilled to be invited to the table. It was happening more and more as she got older and she loved the opportunity to talk with the adults. It made her feel grown up. Even if she didn't have much to contribute, it was still fun to be a part of it. Tonight was different though.

"The only thing I can go on," Rhys continued, "is my instinct. The Holy Spirit. And I'm hearing I should trust him. That's all I've got though and I know I'm asking a lot. Grace and I have talked about it and we feel its worth the risk. We're just counting the days until we're discovered here and if there is someone willing to help us on the outside, we have to take that chance."

The table hung with a silence. Lily watched Wayne and Mary look at each other. Neither really seemed to know what to do. This was the first time Lily had heard about it all, too, so she could understand their feelings. She felt an overwhelming sense of confusion, fear, hope, excitement, and anxiety all at once. She wasn't sure how to process it but she did know that she trusted her parents.

"I think we're gonna have to talk about it," Wayne replied after a long silence. "When are you guys leaving?"

Lily watched her parents look at each other before Grace replied, "Tomorrow night." Lily saw her own shock reflected in the faces of Wayne and Mary.

"Tomorrow." Mary replied. "One day. That's all the time we have to prepare? That's it?"

"I'm sorry," Rhys said, "I meant to tell you sooner but, you know how it is. I didn't have a chance and I couldn't risk explaining anything out there. I had to wait until it was safe so we could plan together if you guys want to come."

Wayne had pulled himself together and was nodding thoughtfully. Mary still looked upset and unsure. Lily was glad to be ignored right now. She didn't know if she would be able to come up with anything worth saying, but was still glad to see her parents interacting like this. It made her proud to see how well they supported each other.

"But we can't. That's just too soon. What about our house? Our stuff? What about our other friends?" Mary was talking fast, almost like she was trying to hold back the inevitable.

Wayne just met her gaze and put a hand on hers. "It'll be OK Mary," Wayne replied. "God provides. God will watch out for us. We'll be OK." Mary grabbed onto his hand as he was talking. Lily watched the fear spread across her face as she realized what he was going to suggest.

Wayne began, "You're right, Rhys. It's only a matter of time before we are discovered here. But I can't put my family through the risk you're suggesting." The tension in the room left with Wayne's decision. Lily noticed that her parents were holding hands under the table while they listened to Wayne's explanation.

"It might be different if I had met this man," Wayne continued. "But, from all I've seen, all we've learned, all we know, I can't blindly trust an outsider. A Rebel. They've killed so many of us, I just can't do it. I will pray for you. I'll pray for your safety and I'll pray that you are right. But I can't put my family through that much risk."

Rhys nodded, meeting Wayne's eyes. "I understand, Wayne. Just know that if we do find something better out there, I'll do what

I can to let you know. I'll come back and get you if I have a chance. But I get it and I respect your decision."

Lily watched the men stand and exchange a hug. Then the women stood up and hugged. They all stood quietly, no one sure quiet what to say. Lily saw the tension building and wanted to break it up before someone suggested stopping for the night. "So," she said quickly, "should we get to studying?" She used the jokiest tone she could think of and it worked.

The room broke out in a quiet laughter as the adults took their seats again. Rhys pulled out a Bible, following the cloth guide so they could pick up where they left off. Lily settled into her chair, filled with thoughts. She listened half heartedly, but was relieved to see the adults settle into their normal patterns, though she did detect a hint of sadness behind their actions. *I suppose this will be our last study,* Lily realized to herself.

That's when it all hit Lily for the first time. She might never see these people again. Craig's smiling face immediately filled her mind. She felt true panic rising in her chest and she fought to control it for the rest of the night. She finally got a short reprieve when the study ended, much later than the usual time, and the adults stood. The women burst into tears and hugged each other. Lily felt some tension release as she burst into tears too. The women pulled Lily into the hug and held each other.

They stayed like that for a long time. When they finally pulled apart, Lily was surprised to see tears running down the men's faces as well. Wayne pulled Mary toward the door, offering a parting wave as they left the building. As soon as the door closed, Rhys pulled both Lily and Grace into a hug. The door opened a second later as Wayne rushed into the room.

Rhys gave Wayne a confused look but realization and shock washed over his face as Wayne rushed down the hall. "We almost forgot the boys!" Mary whispered loudly, as she came back into the room. She was laughing and crying at the same time as Wayne came back, holding a sleeping Charles in his arms.

"Yours is sound asleep," Wayne said to Rhys. Rhys nodded in reply, smiling down at the peaceful, sleeping face of Charles. Wayne held out a hand and Rhys took it. The men held each other's gaze as Wayne said, "May the Lord bless you and keep you. May He cause His face to shine on you and grant you peace. Did I get it right?" Rhys nodded. "Thank you, brother," Wayne continued. "For everything. We love you."

Rhys didn't say anything, he just held the man's hand, tears still running down his face. They broke their shake and Mary followed Wayne out for a second time. Lily was ushered to bed but knew she wouldn't be able to sleep. Craig's face was still filling her mind. *God, please help me see him tomorrow. Let me tell him.* With that, she felt a peace wash over her and was finally able to sleep.

* * *

Lily's heart jumped as she realized she had finally caught his gaze. He met her eyes for a second and she saw a look of concern and confusion cross his face. Then he looked back up front. She was able to pull his gaze several times over the rest of the day and she constantly tried to show the same thing: *I need to talk to you, and I love you, and I'll never see your gorgeous smile again, and I love you, and good bye.* It was a lot to try to express in a single instant. She was pretty sure she just came off looking like she was in pain, but it was the best she could do. And it was working.

Unfortunately she had also pulled the attention of the guard. She could feel him watching her over the past few weeks, ever since he had seen the picture Craig drew. He hadn't said anything, hadn't done anything, but he watched. He was always watching. And his face was showing confusion as well.

The White leading the class hadn't noticed at least, though Lily wasn't sure he would notice much of anything. He was droning on in a monotone face, reading text from the book in front of him, "The many genders expressed by the Whites is a natural progression of our Ascension. Prior to this, the Whites were confused by their inability to match with others in society. Soon, it was realized that their varying expressions were a presentation of their holiness. When several 'gender nonconforming,' as they were called at the time, individuals

Ascended at once, it became clear the Whites are more than others. How much more was obviously not learned for quite some time, but that was one of the first steps on the long path the Whites took to achieve godhood."

Lily's attention waned and she glanced around the room. She met eyes with Craig again and quickly looked away. Then she met eyes with the guard again and felt her heart drop. He had reached some kind of decision. Lily wished she could stop herself, but she couldn't control her face as panic filled her features. She almost jumped out of her chair when the guard said, "I beg your pardon, your Holiness."

Interrupting a White could be considered a capital offense, even when done by Grays. The guard assumed his position of respect and waited for the White to respond. The elderly White, who had just taken a break, turned to look at the Gray. He almost looked lost, like he had forgotten there was anyone else in the room. After a moment he replied, "Yes, my son?"

"I need to remove one of your students from class at this time," the guard said.

The White looked surprised, but then gestured to the room and said, "You may."

The guard stood and put a hand on his heart, looking up and said, "For All Are One."

"And One Serves All, my child," the White replied with a gentle smile. Lily watched as the guard marched to her chair. He put his hand on her arm and she knew there was nothing she could do. She stood and followed the guard. As they passed Craig's chair, the guard stopped for a moment. Then, his voice filled the silence from above her, "And you son, follow me. At attention!"

Craig immediately stood from his chair and offered the older guard a salute. Lily felt Craig step in line behind her. They marched from the room and into the empty street. Lily kept her gaze down, trying hard not to bring any more attention to herself. She had no idea what to expect and felt her breath rising to a panic level as they walked. The guard marched her down the street and through a large metal door into what she had thought was an abandoned building.

He flipped a switch and the room filled with light. The room was mostly bare. The only furniture was a metal table against the far wall with two chairs on either side. The guard pushed her into one of the chairs and pressed her arms onto the table. He grabbed a large metal bar from the wall, and lowered it over the table. Lily placed her arms in the carved space naturally, just to keep her hands from being crushed. The guard locked the bar on the other side of the table, and tightened two straps around her wrists.

Lily felt her panic rising as she realized she was locked in and at the mercy of these two men. She felt a tear roll down her cheek. The guard sat down across from her and stared at her for a minute. The room filled with silence, broken only when Craig cleared his throat.

"Sit," the guard said, pulling out the empty chair next to him. He looked back and forth between the two of them for a moment, before saying with a smile, "So what's going on with the two of you?" Lily had no idea how to answer, so she kept silent and kept her head down.

After a moment, Craig said, "What? What do you mean?"

"Now son, don't play dumb," the guard replied. He put his hand on Craig's shoulder and smiled at him. Lily watched out of the corner of her eye, knowing she couldn't trust the guard. Knowing something bad was going to happen but feeling helpless to react. Whatever happened to her now it was out of her control. Her hands were literally tied.

That's when Lily realized something. It was always out of her control. It was always, all in God's control. God knew what she was going through. Knew what was happening to her and what would happen to her. And He allowed it. He brought her here. And if she was here and in His control, she would be OK. He had suffered and died for her, the least she could do was appreciate and accept that fact. And trust in Him.

Lily felt the tension leaving her body and she finally relaxed. She was able to slow her breathing and keep it under control. She listened as the men continued talking.

"I'm not dumb," Craig replied. "I just don't know what you mean, sir."

The man smiled at Lily and then back to Craig. "I've seen you two. I've been watching you. And her. And the way you look at her. And the way she looks at you. I know that look. And I wanted to help. She looked especially hungry today, so I thought you might want to help her?"

Craig gave a confused look to the guard for a moment, then to Lily. Lily was just as surprised by the guard's change in attitude. And the realization of what he thought finally sank in. *He thinks we want to have sex!* Lily thought to herself.

"Look," the guard continued. He leaned closer to Craig and talked more quietly, "This is a private room. No cameras, nothing. I can give you ten minutes here with her, but you gotta do something for me." The guard met Craig's eyes and seemed to be waiting for a response. Craig just nodded and the guard continued.

"You gotta talk to your dad for me. I've been working this awful post for almost a year. I DeadNamed a White and this post was my punishment. I know, I'm lucky to be alive. Thankfully I had a great service record prior. But I can't take this anymore. Watching kids learn is nothing. I want to be out there. I want my gun back and not this fake. I want to do my part to defend our city again. Shoot some people when they get out of line. You gotta help me."

Lily listened in disgust, growing more nauseous with every word the man said. By the end, he was almost sniveling, begging Craig for help. Lily was relieved to see the same look of disgust on Craig's face. Craig covered it up and then looked at Lily. The guard's head was down still and he offered her a small shrug, before finally replying, "Yeah, I can do that, sir. I don't know how much good it'll do but I'll try."

The guard looked up, a smile filling his face. "You will? Great! Thank you, son." The guard finally looked to Lily, his smile changing into something darker. "You better get to it then. And have fun." The guard winked at Craig before standing and leaving the room.

"Oh, by the way," the guard said at the door. He motioned to Lily's arms, "You might want to leave those on. In my experience, the girls can get pretty feisty. I don't think you'll have a problem with this one, but you never know." He gave Craig a small salute and left, closing the door behind himself.

Lily looked up and met Craig's stare. She realized they were truly alone for the first time ever. Not only alone, but they were *supposed* to be alone. And expected to do something she hadn't even dared fantasize about. Anytime her mind started down that path, she had cut it off. She knew that those darker thoughts were always buried in her mind, but she didn't want to think of Craig like that. She was worried what he would think of her, now. For a brief second, she thought he might kiss her, but he seemed just as shocked as her.

The room filled with silence as they stared at each other. Lily didn't know what to say or do, but she waited for Craig to start. Eventually, he cleared his throat then said, "Um," and that's all it took. With that, the flood gates opened and words started pouring out of Lily's mouth.

She explained everything. She confessed her love for Craig. She told him of her fantasies about them dating and then marrying with a full knowledge of the fact that it could never happen. She told him about how great of an artist he was. She again told him she loved him. And then she told him that she was leaving that night and would never see him again.

She finally got control of herself and stopped. Craig sat in stunned silence, a small smile on his lips. "You love me?" he asked, almost as much to himself as to her. Lily felt another tear run down her cheek as she bit her lip, smiled, and nodded.

"Wow," Craig replied, putting his hands through his hair. "Wow!" He stood from his chair and started pacing, grabbing his lip and smiling to himself. Then he stopped and turned to her saying, "But wait. You're leaving? What do you mean?"

Lily felt her stomach drop as she realized she should not have told him that. It had been drilled in to her since before she could walk, no one leaves. All lives are needed in service of others. Plus it is not safe outside. She felt panic rising in her chest as she met his gaze. He rushed to her side, and put his hand on her shoulder and said, "Hey, hey, hey. It's ok. Don't cry. Don't worry. I'm not gonna tell anyone. It's ok."

He tried to hug her but grunted in frustration at the bar holding her arms down. They both seemed to realize that she was still stuck. He quickly unlocked the bar and undid the straps. She noticed his strong arms as he lifted the bar and freed her arms. She threw them around him and he put his arms protectively around her as they both stood. He held her like that and Lily knew for the first time what her mom must feel being wrapped up by Rhys. She felt her body relax into him and she let herself enjoy that moment. *No wonder they hug so often* Lily thought to herself.

Then she pulled back and looked at him. "Tonight," she said. "My dad found a way out and we are going. I don't know that I'll ever see you again, Craig." His name felt so good on her lips. She smiled at being able to say it, but felt her heart well up at the look of sadness and pain in his eyes.

After a moment of thought, he quickly said, "I'll go with you." Lily was shocked to hear those words, and thought she must have been mistaken. But the look of resolve in his eyes told her otherwise. He meant it. "Yeah, yeah!" he continued. "Yeah. I can do it. I can go with you. I can protect you out there."

Lily felt her heart melt at the thought of being protected by him. "You think?" she asked. She almost didn't want to give herself hope, but she loved the idea. It was almost a dream come true.

"When? Where?" Craig asked quickly.

"Not sure when, but tonight," Lily replied. She felt excitement and hope welling up inside her. "My dad said a few hours after full dark we are going to the Bronze gate. The guard there is going to leave his post for a minute and then we are going out to meet some guy my dad knows. That's all I know."

"That's all I need," Craig replied. "I'll be there. I'll meet you there. Tonight at the Bronze gate." Lily nodded, staring into his eyes. He pulled her into another hug. "By the way," he said quietly into her hair, "I love you, too."

She looked up into his eyes and leaned in. He leaned back and their lips met. If Lily had to explain what she thought heaven would feel like, she would describe that moment.

CHAPTER 16

Rhys looked to his family. They were gathered in the kitchen, waiting. They all sat around the dinner table. Rhys could feel the tension in the air and see the fear and anxiety in their faces. He also saw a brave determination that made him proud. Thomas almost looked excited, like he was on an adventure. Rhys smiled to his son as he roughed up Thomas's hair.

"Do you think it's time?" Grace asked again. Rhys smiled and nodded. He was sure it was too early but he knew they were eager to go. They didn't want to miss it. The group stood, gathered the few things they decided to bring, and went to the front door. Rhys looked through the window into the dark street. He nodded to his wife, who opened the door and ushered the children out.

The waxing moon provided some light, but barely enough to see by. Rhys felt a tension in his shoulders and back. Every dark alley drew his attention. He was scanning everything around him, watching out for any signs of life. He led his family as they walked, quickly and quietly, as close to the buildings as they could. They skirted from shadow to shadow, watching for any other movement. Moving at night was something they were familiar with. They had made trips every other week on their way to Wayne's house for Life Group. This felt markedly different though.

Rhys put his back to the edge of a large, brick building and held up a closed fist. They had practiced some simple signs: stop, forward, back, duck. *Worth it,* Rhys thought to himself as his family stopped and put their backs on the wall next to him. He peered around the corner, looking down the wide street. He could see the light of the central complex. He didn't see any movement, but he didn't know if he'd be able to pick it out against the blinding lights of the complex. The street in front of him was lit as well, though more shadows were present this far away from the complex.

Rhys watched for any signs of movement. He felt in his chest a steady, driving thump coming from the complex. He could hear a deep sound as well, that moved with the thump. He wasn't sure what it was, but it didn't seem to be causing any harm. When he was sure there was no movement, he gestured for his family to duck and follow. Then he crouched and ran.

Being in the light was a terrifying feeling, but it was over in seconds. He didn't hear anything. Didn't see anything. His family reached a similar wall behind a building on the other side of the street. They stood there for a moment, listening for any type of reaction. When nothing happened, they relaxed some. They still had a ways to go, but the most dangerous part was past.

They crouched and worked their way through dark alleys and around small shacks. The shacks in this district were empty. The Whites left them available if new Colors were relocated from neighboring cities. As they moved through, Rhys wondered for the first time why that was. The empty district was patrolled along the outer wall by Grays but not the inside. Rhys got close to the outer wall and motioned for the family to stop. They entered an empty shack, with windows looking out toward the Bronze gate.

Through the window, Rhys had a clear view of the entire street. A light shone onto the street from directly over the wall, casting light inside and outside the complex. Sitting on a metal chair inside the wall, gazing into the complex, was a Gray guard. Behind him was the Bronze gate. Grace looked out the window, glancing at the guard.

Rhys breathed out a sigh of relief that they'd made it in time. He held his finger in front of his face and gestured to the family to duck down. Once they were close by and all low, Rhys began in a whisper, "We wait here. We watch. And when I say it's time, we go. Be ready. Sit against the wall. And be quiet."

The family nodded to him and crawled to the wall. They settled into comfortable positions and looked at him. Rhys nodded and then sat up himself. He was able to see the guard but only the top of his head was sticking out. He figured it wouldn't be noticed in the darkness The rest of this head was concealed by the window frame. He leaned against the wall and watched. And prayed.

Hours passed with no movement. Rhys waited patiently. He was proud of how well his family was waiting. The children were sitting almost perfectly silently, holding one small bag each. They didn't have much but Grace had knitted each of them a small doll when they were young. Lily and Thomas both had their dolls. They also had a change of clothes and were each allowed to fill their pouch with whatever else they wanted.

Both Thomas and Lily were good at collecting seemingly random stuff. Rhys had no idea where they got it from, but it seemed like every week they were coming home with some new item they found that caught their attention. And they always had such an interesting story about it. "This feather came from an angel!" "Dad, this rock fell from heaven!" "This stick was made by God, how could I get ever just throw it away?!"

They made pretty convincing arguments. Rhys could almost never bring himself to make them get rid of it. So these items piled up. Grace would throw them out occasionally, but by that time the item had lost its luster. The kids could still tell the story if reminded, but they barely noticed it once it was gone. They'd moved onto some other item of interest.

Rhys smiled at his son, who was starting to doze off. He met eyes with Grace and mouthed, *I love you* to her. She blew him a kiss back and put her arm around Thomas, allowing him to lean into her chest. He closed his eyes and snuggled up to his mother. Rhys looked to Lily and realized something was off.

Lily was looking around, as if waiting for something. She leaned up and looked out the window. Rhys realized she was looking for something else. Waiting for something else. He looked around, glancing up and down the street. When he didn't see or hear anything, he turned back to Lily. She continued her erratic searches and behavior. He tried to meet her eye, but she seemed to be avoiding looking at him.

Rhys was about to crawl over to Lily, when he heard a sound from the street. He looked out the window and saw a short, dark figure step into the light from the street. The Gray guard hadn't noticed him yet, but he was peeking at the gate. Rhys realized another person looked to be escaping with them. He couldn't believe how brazen they were being though, standing in the street like that. He watched as the figure slowly started moving forward.

Rhys looked back to Lily and saw her staring at the figure through the window. Her eyes were glowing and she had a radiant smile on her face. Rhys looked back to the figure and noted for the first time the Gray uniform. He looked at the face of a young man, who was searching the darkness for something. He looked back to his daughter and knew he was searching for her. She must have spoken to him, maybe even planned this.

"Looks like I'll be meeting the boyfriend," he whispered very quietly. Lily didn't answer but beamed at her dad. She nodded and her eyes filled with tears. Rhys sighed to himself then looked back to the street. He was trying to decide if he should go help the boy, or wait for him to find his own cover when the guard stood.

They Gray reached his arms over his head in an over emphasized stretch before saying out loud to the empty street, "Well, time to take a leak." Rhys looked back to his family, heart racing as he watched the guard leave his post. The guard walked down the street and around the corner. The gate was open. Rhys looked back at his family and nodded. He had just stood up when the alarm sounded.

Every light on the street turned on, flooding the city with light. Rhys ducked down quickly, hiding out of sight of the window. A blaring alarm continued ringing, drowning out all noise in the city. Rhys poked his head back up and watched as the confused guard rushed to his post. The guard grabbed a small box and held it to his mouth. Rhys watched as he did that a few times, looking around the street. The complex was filled with light and noise.

Rhys looked down the street, trying to find the young man again. He was crouched between two houses, peeking around the corner. He seemed to be panicked, unsure what to do or where to go.

The alarm cut off and silence echoed in Rhys's ears. He could see the guard talking but couldn't make out any words.

The guard stepped up and looked down the street. Then he brought up his gun as he said in a loud voice, "You there! Come out or I will shoot!"

Rhys thought the guard was yelling at him for a second, so he held perfectly still. The guard continued looking down the street, though and Rhys realized the young man had been seen. The man stepped out with his hands up. He walked into the center of the street and stood at attention, his Gray uniform standing out against the dirty buildings around him.

Rhys watched as the older man called the young man up. The young man rushed to the older man and stood at his side. After a few minutes, more Grays came rushing down the street. A Gray woman hugged the young man to her chest, the boy's parents Rhys assumed. Rhys could hear the angry tones but couldn't make out any of the words. The young man was escorted away by his mother and father.

After they left, the Gray guard resumed his post but was now accompanied by three more Grays. The lights turned out again and the guards stood at their post. All of them were talking and laughing. Rhys wasn't sure what to do, so he waited. After a few minutes, he peeked out again and saw that one of the Grays had climbed the wall and was looking out beyond the gate. The buildings around the complex had been destroyed, leaving an open expanse that could be more easily monitored. The guard brought up his gun and fired a series of shots, seemingly at random.

Rhys watched as the man gestured to a younger guard below. The man on the wall was laughing and pointing out, gesturing to the crumbling buildings Rhys was just able to see in the distance. The young man dropped his shoulders and walked out the gate. Rhys could see the man's flashlight bobbing as he made his way through the stretch of cleared land. Soon the man came back and held up something to the other Grays. Rhys was just barely able to make out the large cross necklace that had been worn by the strange man he met in the forest.

Rhys lowered his head and gestured to his family to move toward the back door. Nothing more could be done except leave. Lily was crying, Grace and Thomas were quietly solemn, and Rhys was determined to come try again. They had almost gotten out and the man said every Sunday. *But that was HIS cross* Rhys thought to himself. Would there be anyone waiting if they tried again? Rhys tried to keep a hope of being saved alive as they slowly and carefully worked their way back home.

CHAPTER 17

R hys was awakened from a fitful sleep. He rubbed his eyes, trying to clear his head and decipher what had been dream from what was real. The trip through the city last night, attempting to escape certainly felt like a dream. But he knew it was real. And he knew it hadn't worked. He was sitting up out of bed when he realized what woke him up was the sound of loud voices yelling outside.

"A raid!" Rhys whispered urgently to Grace before jumping out of bed. He ran to his children's room to help them prepare and double check their room. He and Grace were very careful about what they allowed their children to have displayed. The severity of the consequences made Rhys double check every time. Better safe than sorry. It had been months since the last raid. A lot of time to accumulate things.

He scanned his eyes over Lily's side of the room, relieved to see bare floor and walls. He told her to get dressed quickly and meet in the living room. Rhys heard Grace moving things around in their room as she did her search. He turned and looked to Thomas's bed. Thomas was already up and getting dressed. Rhys scanned his son's bed and walls quickly. His eyes landed on the end of a small stick, poking out from under Thomas's pillow.

Rhys felt his heart drop at what they had nearly missed. He lifted the pillow and pulled out a cross made out of two sticks tied together with thread. Thomas looked from the cross to his dad's eyes, panic and terror covering his face. Rhys sighed out relief and broke the thread before pulling Thomas into a hug.

"It's OK, bud," Rhys said quietly. Thomas gasped into Rhys's chest, doing his best to hold back tears. "Is there anything else?" Rhys asked.

"No, Dad. No. I swear." Thomas replied quickly. "I knew that was there, and I was gonna break it, but I just didn't have time yet." Rhys knew that his son was telling the truth. He tried to slow his heart and control his breathing as he held his son a moment longer.

"I'm glad we got it," Rhys said. "Now go to the living room. I'll be out in a minute." Rhys heard the voices growing closer. There would be a knock at their door any minute now. Rhys rushed Thomas out of the room after making one last quick scan. He joined his wife and daughter in the living room, double checked those spaces including the table and rug, and then stepped out into the street.

The street was filled with other Colors, all looking disheveled. Rhys and his family did their best to imitate the blank stare on the faces of most Colors around them. A large group of Gray guards worked their way down the street, moving from shack to shack. One of the leaders sat on top of a horse, surveying the entire street. He had a rifle over the pommel of his horse and an angry look in his eyes. Rhys had to stop himself from gasping as he recognized the necklace hanging in the guard's hand. It was the same necklace he'd seen on the man in the forest. The same necklace he'd seen last night. He quickly brought his attention back to his home and away from the Gray. His mind filled with possibilities of how they had gotten that cross, the most obvious being that they had killed the man.

The Grays were loud as they yelled their instructions, but the Colors moved silently. No one offered a fight or protest in any way. They all knew what it would mean to object. They kept their heads down and waited silently in the street, barely acknowledging each other. A few houses down, Rhys saw Wayne and Mary walk out of their house, holding Charles's hand. Rhys nodded subtly to Wayne as they met each other's gaze. Wayne gave Rhys a small smile and shrug as he melted into the crowd. Their attention was drawn to the Gray on horseback as when he started yelling.

"An atrocity has been committed!" he yelled out. "A rebel was found out of our walls last night, attempting to sneak into the

Complex. He was discovered with a jar of poison. A colorless, tasteless poison that is capable of killing a man with a single drop. His plan was to poison our water supply in an attempt to kill as many of our beloved Whites as possible. This is the hatred the rebels show for us."

The Colors on the street had turned to face the man, all keeping their heads down but listening attentively. "As if that wasn't bad enough," the man lifted his arm, openly displaying the cross, "this was also found on his person!" The Colors looked up as expected and then shrank back in fear. Some women literally yelled out, falling to the ground. Men started shouting out sounds of anger, each trying to be louder than the next.

The Gray held up his other hand and the crowd fell silent. "Now," the Gray continued once he was sure the Color's outburst had subsided. They all stared in rapt attention. "We obviously have to figure out who in here was helping this man. He could not have done it alone and we know someone in these very walls was complicit."

At this, several people in the crowd began yelling out: "No!" "It wasn't us!" "Not here! It couldn't be!" People began attempting to shift blame in any direction they could. "District 5! That's where the real bad people are!" "Have you looked in District 2?" "District 1 is horrible!" The Gray let this go on for a minute, listening to the voices of the people and smiling. The other Grays continued searching each house. Rhys felt his pulse rise as he noticed his house was one away from being searched. He turned his attention back to the Gray as he continued talking.

"Have no fear, we will of course find the culprit and remove it to keep you safe. Anyone willing to even touch this hideous thing," the Gray said, holding up the cross in his gloved hand, "is obviously a danger to you all. You never know what someone like that could do. We know what they've done in the past. The atrocities committed by the followers of this symbol. I need not tell you how deadly this cross is."

With that, the Gray started walking his horse, making his way to the next block to deliver a similar speech. Following behind him was a Gray sergeant on foot. He surveyed the privates, who were doing the actual searching. Grays came to him with things of interest they had found in the shacks. These items were piled in a box by the privates and presented to the sergeant. With each box, the Gray leader would pick through the box, looking briefly at each item. Periodically he would toss an item over his shoulder, to be picked up by a younger private following behind him. These items were then loaded into carts to be destroyed.

Rhys jumped as a Gray standing in front of his home said, "Who's house is this? Step forward!" He put his arm around Grace and Lily and stepped forward, Grace gently guiding Thomas with them. None of them looked up at the guard and they didn't say a word as the Grays entered their home. After a few minutes, one of the men came out holding a box. Rhys watched as the sergeant looked through their items, a book, some thread and a needle, and their name sheet. When he read their name, he looked up at Rhys and Grace. The sergeant nodded to himself, pushed the box back into the hands of the waiting Gray, and stepped toward Grace.

Grace felt a moment of panic as she recognized Sergeant Jones. He placed a firm hand on her upper arm and pulled her away from Rhys. She wanted to fight but knew to object would mean death. Jones started walking, pulling Grace along beside him. She looked over her shoulder and made eye contact with Rhys. He had a look of fear and shock in his eyes, but that lessened when she met his eyes. Rhys mouthed *I love you*, and tried for a smile. Grace replied with *I love you* and was relieved very slightly to see Rhys's strong arms around her children's shoulders. Lily had her face pressed to Rhys's shirt and Thomas looked up as his father in fear and confusion. Grace knew her kids were in good hands if something happened, and that gave her some strength.

She silently prayed to God for strength enough to endure whatever was happening and protection for both her and Rhys. She was pulled roughly into the house.

* * *

"Clear out," Jones said loudly. The younger Grays in the room stopped what they were doing, with looks of confusion on their faces. "NOW!" the man yelled. The privates jumped, dropped what they were doing, and hurried out of the room. Grace watched as the older man shut the door and stepped toward her. She stood with her head down and hands clasped behind her back. He grabbed her arm and pulled her into the kitchen, out of sight of the window. Grace felt a moment of relief at seeing the undisturbed rug under the table.

Once alone, Jones surveyed her kitchen, a look of disgust on his face. He made her wait in silence. Grace thought she knew where this was going and was physically preparing her body for what might come. She realized that she was crying and tried to make herself stop. The man continued looking around the room in silence for a full minute.

"I got something for ya," he finally said. Grace almost jumped at the sudden sound. She wasn't sure how to respond, so she waited. Jones unbuckled his belt and unbuttoned his pants. He pulled out the waist line and then reached into his pants. He pulled out a small, white bag and held it out for Grace.

She recognized it as a packet of seeds. She almost smiled in relief as she stepped forward. Just as she reached out for it, Jones pulled it out of her reach. "Now, now," he said with a smile, "not so fast. Guy that gave this to me said you had to earn it." Grace felt her stomach turn as she saw the look in his eyes. He stepped toward her and grabbed her forearms.

She could only stand and allow it to happen as she felt his strong, firm grip. She knew he was far too strong for her. And even if by some miracle, she was able to fight him off, she would immediately be killed for attacking a Gray. She had no option but to go along with whatever he had in mind. He held her like that for a moment, staring into her eyes. She met his gaze with a look of fear, waiting for some indication as to what he wanted her to do. His eyes slid down her body, taking in her form. She could see the hunger filling his gaze.

She did the only thing she could think to do. She prayed. She prayed that God would soften this man's heart. Help him see that he still had a choice. He could still do the right thing and stop this. She prayed harder than she could ever remember praying, not just for her safety but for this man's soul.

As the moment stretched, she realized his gaze was changing, ever so slowly. He met her eyes as she prayed. His hunger shifted to confusion as he stared at her. Grace could feel the presence of the Holy Spirit and felt herself filled with peace, comfort, and strength. She did all she could to make her face say: *you don't have to hurt me.* And she was shocked to find Jones's gaze softening. He closed his eyes and shook his head, turning away from her. He let her hand go and stepped back into the view of the street. He glanced out the window, watching the Grays in their continued search.

He blinked a few times, looking from her, out the window at the chaos on the street, and back to her. He looked confused for a second, but pulled himself back together. He took a deep breath and pulled his shoulders back before stepping toward Grace and back into the privacy of the kitchen. He handed the small packet of seeds over to Grace. She took it without any resistance. Jones was not looking at her, but had turned back and was walking to the door. He took a deep breath and reached up to open it when a loud voice rang out in the street.

"SIR! WE FOUND SOMETHING!"

CHAPTER 18

⌒⌢⌒

Grace was left alone in her home as Jones rushed out of the building. She followed close behind, not quite sure what to do. She joined the crowd in the street, looking toward the commotion. They were all facing a young Gray standing tall, holding a small boy by the arm. Grace felt her heart drop when she realized it was Charles. She put her arm around Rhys's waist and pulled her body close to his. She looked up and met his panicked expression.

"What is going on here," Jones's loud voice rang out, bringing the entire crowd to silence.

"Sir, we found something," the younger Gray replied. He stood at attention with his hand on his forehead and feet together. He waited quietly for a response from the older man.

"Well, what is it?" Jones said.

"This boy, he is acting suspicious," the private said. Grace could see Jones's shoulders visibly drop. Grace was not sure what was happening but really wished Charles could be standing next to his parents and not alone with the Grays.

"Suspicious..." Jones replied. His voice dripped with sarcasm and annoyance.

"Yes, sir," the young man stammered. He was still standing at attention, but his pose wavered slightly. "Suspicious. I thought you might want to know. Talk to him. Maybe."

Jones rolled his eyes and then looked down at the boy. This was the first time Grace had really looked at Charles too. She was shocked and scared at what she saw. His face was etched with anger and determination. He looked resolved and strong. Grace would not have expected a fourteen year old capable of looking so grown up. He stared directly into the eyes of Jones, not allowing his gaze to waver once. Grace felt her stomach drop as Charles held the look.

Grace wanted to bury her face in Rhys's shoulder, but couldn't stop herself from watching the scene unfold. Jones pulled his shoulders back and stood tall. It seemed to Grace he was watching the crowd out of the corner of his eye, but was trying not to actually look at anyone. Jones seemed genuinely uncomfortable. "Alright then," Jones said before he took a short, deep breath. "Boy, come here."

The private finally let go of Charles's arm as he pushed the young man forward. Charles was able to stay on his feet but he stumbled. When he stood, his shoulders were thrown back farther than the older man standing in front of him. Jones sighed and crouched down, bringing his eyes to level with the boy. "What is your name, son?" Jones asked.

Charles held his gaze a moment before replying, "Charles."

"OK, Charles, and what do you know? You obviously know something or you wouldn't be standing here right now. Wouldn't be looking at me like that. So, what do you know?" Jones finished and stared straight at Charles, maintaining his bent posture.

"Well, sir," Charles began. "I know one thing that you don't." The entire street was silent, listening to the boy's words. "I know that Jesus Christ is my Lord and Savior." He ended the sentence projecting his voice loud enough for the entire street to hear. Immediately his arms were pulled behind his back and he was pinned against two guards.

Jones had jumped up and started shouting in response, trying to overpower the smaller voice, "No! No! No! That name will not be uttered within these walls."

The crowd had all heard. Grace was shocked to see people whispering quietly to each other. She watched Jones survey the Colors around him with a look of fear on his face. She could see the man's thoughts churning as he tried to come up with a way to regain control. Unfortunately for him, that choice was taken from him when Charles started shouting again.

"If my Lord were as powerless as you say, would the Whites need to silence Him like this? We worship the Whites, can worship the buddha, gods of hindu, mohamed. We can worship who we choose so long as we place the Whites first. The one name we cannot utter is the name of Jesus. Have you wondered why that is?"

The crowd listened in awed silence. To hear this coming from the mouth of a child was so strange to almost be unbelievable. But many heads in the crowd were nodding. And more with each word. Grace felt a small fire of hope fill her chest at seeing the look in the eyes of the people around her. She even saw a few Grays nodding in a thought and agreement.

Jones had regained his composure. He looked to the street with a sly smile before answering, "I shouldn't encourage this, but your question has such an obvious answer it will be worth sharing before you are taken. Your God is the only that preaches of hate. The only name shouted when the Whites were oppressed prior to their ascension. Your God condemned them for things they could not control. For their sexuality. For their expression. Your God had no care for the planet or the people in it and condemned women to suffer with children they were not able to provide for. Your God forced all women to carry to term, forcing more children to be born, contributing to further harm to the planet."

Grace felt her hope die as the crowd reacted to the man's words. Their thoughtful looks devolved into apathy or anger as they watched Jones talk. When he had finished, the crowd stood in silence, letting the words echo off the walls.

Charles looked up at Jones and then at the Colors around him with sympathy. He replied, "You're right. My God is the only who knows us. Who sees us for the sinners that we are. And the only God that wants us to be better. To do better. My God knows what we need to be happy. To that end, my God wants all people to follow His laws. He wants us to find true, lasting, fulfilling happiness. Joy. True meaning. True life. When we follow Him, we gain that life. When we turn away from Him, we suffer, and God does not want us to suffer.

"So, why is my God the only God who judges? Because he's the only God who truly loves and the only God who cares. Cares so much He sent is one and only Son, Jesus, to die for my sins. To rescue me and bring me to etern-"

The boy's voice was cut off. While he was speaking, Jones had instructed the guard holding him to strike. A fist smacked into Charles's face with a wet thud. The silence hanging over the crowd was deafening. All eyes seemed to be on Jones, waiting for him to respond. Waiting to be told what to do. Jones looked down and sighed, knowing that he had no alternative.

After a moment Jones looked up and called out, "Who are this boy's parents?" Wayne and Mary stepped forward. Jones walked up to them, looking them up and down. Wayne smiled sadly at his son, but Grace knew him well enough to see the pride in Wayne's eyes. And the acceptance. Grace looked for Mary's face but she had it buried in Wayne's shoulder.

Jones continued, "So, what are we going to find in your house?"

Wayne looked over the crowd, a serene smile on his face. Grace watched as Wayne's gaze met Rhys's eyes. The men shared a moment and each gave a small nod. Then Wayne kissed his wife's head and stepped forward. He said loudly, "Salvation in Jesus Christ!"

Jones ran up and struck Wayne in the face, dropping him to the ground. He motioned to the Grays standing silently around the crowd, then jumped and ran into the house. They Grays didn't seem entirely sure what to do. A few followed Jones into the shack. Others looked to each other and then raised their guns, pointing at the crowd. Wayne lay on the ground and Grace was shocked to hear him laughing. Loudly and wildly.

"Thank you, Jesus!" Wayne yelled to the sky. "Thank You and forgive them! Soften the hearts of those here that they might see the truth of Your light."

Jones ran out of the house and kicked Wayne in the face, silencing the man. A spray of blood flew into the air and onto the colorful, dirty clothing of those nearest. Mary leapt to her husband's side, raising a protecting arm over their heads.

Jones towered above the couple, holding a small, dark book high above his head. "Blasphemers!" he shouted into the air. The crowd began screaming out in fear of the book and yelling accusations of heresy at Wayne and Mary. Grace watched it all in horrified silence. She held more tightly to Rhys's hand, who squeezed her back. They made eye contact for a brief second, but their attention was drawn back to Jones as he continued.

"Where did you get this?" Jones said. The street had gone silent moments before when Jones held up a closed fist. All were listening and watching, waiting for the cue from Jones to show their devoutness. No Color wanted to be declared sympathetic toward Christians so all were ready to show just how angry they were at Wayne and Mary's blasphemy.

Wayne looked up and was quiet for a second. Then he shook himself and stood from the ground. He raised his chin, holding himself in a strong, proud pose. Mary stood beside him, one arm over his chest as he put a protective arm over her shoulder. When he was ready he replied loudly, "I found it salvaging and was able to sneak it home."

"Who else has seen this?" Jones asked loudly.

"No one," Wayne replied quickly and loudly.

"Well," Jones replied, "I would certainly hope not. Were any of you good people around us to know of this book, I'm sure any one of you would have turned this man in as a hateful, spiteful, Christian, right?"

At Jones's words, the crowd erupted in yelling at him, "We had no idea!" "We would have told someone right away." "He's a monster!" "We never knew!"

The crowd quieted when a man stepped forward and said, "I saw him praying but I was too scared to report it! Those Christians can make it rain fire and I didn't want to hurt our holy Whites!" The crowd mumbled their agreement and then fell into a hushed quiet when Jones held up his hands.

"I believe you, good citizens," Jones said with a smile. "This man was obviously working alone and none of you knew." Grace could feel the crowd relax. Jones let the moment hang for a minute before continuing, "But...now that you know, it is quite the dishonor for your district." Grace looked up at his words and saw a malicious smirk.

"I mean, the boy will obviously be crucified for his words," Jones said almost offhandedly. The guards holding him immediately began walking him toward the Worship Hall. There hadn't been a crucifixion in over a year, but the crosses stood always ready if needed.

Grace felt herself filled with revulsion. A thought filled her head and she heard herself whisper, "They shouldn't be able to hide it." Rhys looked down to her and met her eyes. She was filled with anger, bordering on wrath. The idea of Charles's body hanging hidden away in the same place their ears were filled with lies each night was more than Grace could bear at the moment. It felt like the worst injustice. She felt her anger sweeping into Rhys.

Grace watched as Rhys said loudly, "Your pardon, sir." He seemed almost surprised to have spoken. Grace nodded and Rhys continued, "Need he be crucified so far away? Wouldn't it be a better reminder to us were he crucified here? I would like to prove the allegiance of our district by building a new cross here. In a place we can all see it every day. This young man will be the first and only to be crucified on it."

Jones appeared taken aback. His mouth opened and closed a few times before he said, "A noble gift. Yes, I believe that would be better." At his words, Rhys ran over to a pile of wood stacked inside the outer wall of the Complex to gather supplies. Jones didn't seem to know how to handle it but allowed it to happen.

As the crowd waited, they began whispering together in small groups. Jones jumped and seemed to realize that he had almost lost their attention. "But," he began loudly. He let the silence ring for a minute, ensuring the Colors were listening again. "But, what of these two?" The Colors looked to Wayne and Mary, who stood almost forgotten off to the side.

"This man brought a forbidden book into your midst. A dangerous book that put all of your lives at risk. If a White were to have seen this book, who knows how many of you we would be ordered to strike down in punishment? Are you going to let this transgression go unchallenged?"

The crowd began yelling in response, "No!" "Of course, not!" "Those heathens deserve death!" Jones let the crowd noise go on for a while before putting up his hands. When the crowd was silent, he said, "Well then. It sounds like you already have an idea, so I'll trust you to follow through."

The crowd began moving as one toward Wayne and Mary. Grace didn't move. She tried not to be pulled forward as the crowd moved around her. Some Colors picked up rocks but most just clenched their fists as they surrounded the couple. Wayne stood tall, hugging his wife against his body.

Before the first strike landed, Wayne shouted out: "May God have mercy on you all." He then pulled Mary into a kiss as he was pummeled. They fell to the ground, still holding each other. They didn't yell out, but Grace could hear their grunts of pain as they were struck repeatedly. Her stomach churned and she looked up, right into the eyes of Jones. Grace was shocked to see sadness in his eyes as he looked at her.

At that moment, while the blows were still landing on Wayne and Mary, Rhys lifted the large cross. Grace was shocked that he had put it together so quickly. The cross stood solidly on the street as Rhys walked back to Grace. He looked to Jones as two privates lifted Charles. They tied his arms to the side bars of the cross.

Charles looked ahead and saw his parents being killed. He shouted out, "Father, forgive them! My God, please welcome them to Your loving arms. Usher them through your holy gates!"

"Shut up!" Jones said. Grace could see the fury on his face.

Charles didn't stop, though. "I see Your shining face God. Thank You for blessing me with this chance and for welcoming me into Your embrace."

"Shut up! Shut up! Shut up!" Jones was repeatedly yelling. He had pulled out his gun and was pointing it toward Charles.

"Your love for us knows no bounds," Charles continued. He was smiling joyfully, looking up toward heaven, arms outstretched on the cross. This didn't seem to be hindering his speech at all. He continued, "Thank you for the offer of Salvation. Thank you for seeing the value in all life and allowing us to be better. Showing us the way to be better. And I pray that You open the eyes of those bearing witness to what is happening today. Show them the beauty of Your love and glory. The light, peace, joy, and goodness that comes from following Your word. Thank You, God for Your wonderful plan for me. For using me to further Your glor-"

A loud shot echoed through the street. Charles's voice fell silent. The crowd, all of whom had stopped hitting Wayne and Mary to listen to Charles's words, tuned to stare at Jones. He kept his gun pointed at Charles, whose head had fallen against his chest and was swaying side to side. The first drops of blood fell from Charles's hair. The crowd stepped back, leaving Wayne and Mary.

Grace was shocked to see that they were still breathing with wet, ragged coughs. Jones sighed when he saw that as well. He turned his gun and shot each of them in the back. The entire street fell silent. The Colors were looking down, not wanting to see or be seen by anyone. Jones let out a long, deep sigh and then said, "Well, that was that. Off to work."

The Colors jumped and each rushed into their houses to get ready for work. Rhys grabbed Grace and ushered the kids through the door. Closing it behind himself. He stared in shock, unsure what to do. He looked at the faces of his kids, who were barely holding themselves together. Rhys saw they needed him, so he said a quick prayer for strength and then ushered the family into the kitchen. Once out of sight of the window, he pulled them all into a hug.

"Daddy," Lily said through sobs. "Daddy, how could God let them do that? How did God let that happen?" Rhys pulled her head into his shoulder and wrapped his arms around her. Grace pulled away and crouched down to hug Thomas, both listening.

"Honey," Rhys began, making sure to keep quiet enough that they wouldn't be overheard. "Honey, it's easy to trust God when things are good, right? When we are fed and comfortable. Not happy living here but content and free of suffering." He pulled away, and looked into his daughter's eyes. Thomas and Grace were listening attentively as well.

Rhys continued, "When it's like that, trusting God is easy. Our true test of our faith in God is times like now. Times when we don't understand and can't understand. Can we trust God in the midst of suffering? Can we still lean on God? Can we believe that what He either did or allowed will be used for good? Can we still follow Him? Because, if we can, He will use our lives to do wonderful, powerful, amazing things.

"So," Rhys continued, "why did God let them do that? I don't know. Not right now anyways. But I know that God has a plan for it and that His plan is good." Rhys stopped talking and pulled his family into another hug. "But, right now? This hurts. And we need to be with that pain for a while. I promise you, it will get better over time. But it takes a long time. And while you are waiting, your mother and I will always be here to help. To remember, to laugh, and to talk about our times with them. Then they're never really gone, they'll always be a part of us so long as we remember and honor them."

Rhys looked to his family and smiled. "And we know that it isn't good-bye forever, right? It's just a see you later. They are preparing a place for us with Jesus and God. They are watching over us now, eager to see us again." Lily smiled at that and wiped the tears away from her eyes. She nodded to herself and went to her room to get dressed. Thomas followed close behind.

Once the kids were gone, Grace smiled sadly at him and pulled him in for a kiss. They held that kiss for a very long time. They shared in each other's loss and sadness. Shared their grief. But also shared their comfort. They were each a rock for the other, weathering the storm together.

"Oh, by the way," Grace said. She pulled out the seed packet and continued, "I've probably only got just a couple of weeks until I'm gonna be found out. Anything less than two weeks old, you won't be able to tell the difference. But, if he's watching, which I'm sure he is, he'll be able to tell soon." She sighed and put her head against his shoulder.

"Well that settles it," Rhys said as if coming to a final decision. "I was on the fence about trying again, but next Sunday. Next Sunday we leave."

CHAPTER 19

Lily sat silently in class, doing her best to hold back tears. Thoughts of Charles kept jumping to the surface of her mind. The joy in his face when he finally beat her at Go. His deep belly laugh when she would tickle him. The surprised and proud look in his eyes the first time he was able to pin her when they were wrestling. *He was such a good kid*, she thought to herself. She realized for the first time that he wasn't much younger than her. He had always felt like a little brother.

She brought her attention back to the front when the guard stepped to attention. The droning voice of the White "teaching" stopped and the room fell to silence, all waiting expectantly. She just wasn't sure what she was waiting for. After a minute, a second White slowly entered the room and stepped up to the podium.

"You will all follow me," she said quietly and turned. They all watched in silence as she slowly left the room. Their usual teacher stepped into line behind, followed by the White students. They walked at a slow even pace, keeping their heads up and their noses in the air.

After they left the room, the Grays stood from their seats and saluted. At a command from their leader, they all trotted into line and then followed the Whites. The Colors were quick to rise once the room was empty. The Colors hadn't been given any clear instructions, which meant they were supposed to know what do to. None of them did, however. So what happened was a few clusters of sheepish people moving staggerdly down the street. Keeping close enough to the Grays to maintain respect but not so close to draw attention to any one person.

Lily found herself in this group, surrounded by her classmates. She looked over her shoulder and realized the entire school was following. She was in the oldest class, so the younger students were looking to her class for guidance. Lily wished she knew what was expected of them. Each time she moved forward, she felt the other students of her class following. Someone had to be out front and Lily knew no one else would volunteer. She could feel the eyes of people in the nearby buildings on her. As the group moved, several window shutters closed.

Lily did her best to not draw attention to herself though. She had her head bowed and was always careful not to be out front for long. She would take a few tentative steps then stop, allowing the quiet mass of people to move around her. Then she shifted direction slightly and moved out front again, causing almost a leap frog effect of the Color students. She felt her pulse quicken when she realized where they were going.

They turned and she saw the cross in the distance. She couldn't see his figure but knew Charles would still be on it. To her surprise, when the cross came into view, she could only see wood. The cross was empty. Lily felt a crazy moment of hope that Charles was still alive. Or alive again. She knew it was ridiculous, but couldn't stop the thought.

The Grays had taken up posts along the street and the Whites were standing in front of the empty cross. Lily knew what was expected at this point. She bowed her head and quickly assumed the position of worship. She dropped to her knees and planted her face on the ground, arms extended in front of her head. She listened as the other Colors around her followed her lead.

Once everyone was in position, the street was silent. Lily could hear the wind move through the street. She even heard a bird calling out from above. Then the White spoke.

"I've gathered you here, lowered myself to address you within your own district so I can speak to you. We have been informed of an incident that occurred in this very spot this morning. Some of you may know of what I speak, but I know not all of you were there. Your great and holy Whites felt that, since not all were able to bear witness to the dire event that occurred here today. We felt that all would benefit from an accurate account of the incident. We want to make sure all know the truth so the lies spouted could be corrected, rather than take root in the soft, weak minds of the Colors.

"A young, Color boy, full of hatred and anger, spoke out against the Whites. Knowing that his words would cause pain and anguish to your gods, he spoke of his devotion to an old god of evil. A god whose followers ridiculed, mocked, attacked, and eventually slaughtered my ancestors. A god who demanded purity and hated all those who dared stand against him. We all know this god was eventually defeated, leading to the Ascension.

"And yet, this young man continued to spout hatred and lies! He may have tainted the minds of any who heard him, causing his hate filled, evil message to spread like a virus." The White paused for a moment as she looked over the faces of the students. Lily didn't have to fake her fear and noted a general feeling of dread amongst those around her.

She continued, "I thought you all could use a history lesson. A reminder of the dangers of this symbol. This very cross was a symbol of their hatred. The fact that they used a form of torture as their main symbol should tell you all you need know about their faith. The things their believers were willing to do at any time. In any place. The followers of that old god would burn any they thought deserving on a cross just like this. The truth didn't matter. Those accused had no chance to object. No chance for grace or mercy.

"People were burned for any number of offenses. Homosexual or transsexual? You were just trying to bring more love into the world and they called you perverted. Black? You were burned just for your skin color. Woman willing to speak her mind? You were burned as a witch. And once the evil Christian morals had decayed to the point of burning people, the cross became a symbol of their faith. A reminder for them to hate. A reminder that any people Christians designated as 'other' were deserving of death.

"After years of torture by Christians, the Ascension finally provided the Whites a way to fight back. Our true nature was revealed and the evil god was overcome. The Grays of today were the first to worship, granting strength and power to the Whites and stripping power from that evil god of old. Once weakened, the Christians were defeated and subjugated by the Grays. The Grays were able to protect their new gods. And those of you who weren't brave enough to step up in the defense of our Whites continue to pay for the debts of your ancestors.

"But, the Whites are very generous. Any Color who has shown sufficient reverence can earn their Grays. All Colors should put forth intentional effort into finding ways to earn attention and credits. Enough credits can be traded for temporary Grays, which will allow any of you a chance to prove yourself worthy. Now, while this cross burns," as she stepped away, she dropped a match and the entire cross leapt up in flames. The class was caught by surprise and some let out shrieks of fear.

"...we will worship for the remainder of your class time." The White stepped up to a podium that had been haphazardly built on the street and the Color students bowing their head began the chant of worship. It was very familiar to them, though they usually only did it once at the beginning of their nightly worship. They still had hours left of class time. Lily sighed softly as she realized she would be continuing the chant for the entire afternoon.

She felt the heat from the burning cross pressing against her back. With a jolt she remembered Charles's dead body hanging on that cross. She felt revulsion followed by anger rising in her stomach as she thought about the words of the White. The lies she had told. Lies about what Charles had said and lies about the history of the Christians. She'd looked in her dad's Bible and saw it was published almost seventy years ago. That was way before the Christians had started attacking in their stories told during worship each night. And yet, her older Bible had a cross on it. The cross must mean something more and the Whites were corrupting it. They were lying about it and using the cross for their own power.

I promise, Charles, Lily thought to herself. *I promise I won't forget you. And I'll do whatever I can to continue the fight.* As she continued chanting, she found her mind wandering again to Charles. But instead of pain, she felt rage now. Anger at the White for lying and anger at those in her city who allowed this to happen. The anger covered her pain, though not completely. She felt a tear slide down her nose and splash onto the dirt in front of her.

CHAPTER 20

G race felt her pulse racing as she walked into the Gardens. She kept her head down, but felt sweat beading up on her brow. She knew she wasn't the only one, but she also knew that it was abnormal for her. If any of the Grays paid close enough attention they would see that she was behaving differently. They would know that something was happening and could question her on the spot. She prayed that no one was that dutiful to their work.

She followed the Color in front of her, walking with her head down in single file with the other Colors. They peeled off one at a time as they got to their workstation. Grace stepped up to her table, feeling the packet of seeds pressed against her lower leg. She had worked with Rhys not even an hour ago to figure out how to get the seeds in. They'd used a scrap of old clothing to tie the packet to her leg, at about mid calf. Once it was in place, she had chosen her most intact dress to wear for the day. Her plan was to wait until just before she was given seeds to plant. When they started coming around the room with seeds, she would pretend to drop something. Once on the ground, she could reach to her dress and grab the packet. From there, she had no idea what would happen.

She felt her pulse rising again as she thought about how terrible her plan was. She had no idea what to do from there. She felt herself losing control of her breathing. The thought of standing with the packet when the Grays stopped at her table made her freeze in fear. She looked around the room, feeling her eyes filling with tears. She seemed to have forgotten how to breathe. Her heart was hammering in her chest. Her legs felt weak and a cold sweat broke out over her.

She scanned the room and then her attention was drawn up to the open window. She felt the warmth of the sun on her face. She closed her eyes and took a deep breath through her nose. In that breath she smelled the room, the flowers, the dirt, the life held in that room. She breathed out and took another deep breath, savoring the fresh scents around her.

She remembered that God made everything around her. God helped the plants grow. God was in the room with her. Her heart slowed. She still didn't have a plan but she knew that God was with her. God was in control. And God would help her through whatever she needed to do. She said a thank you prayer to God as she looked down to her table, feeling much more in control and at ease.

A small bell rang out and she started her shift. The morning passed with surprising monotony. Grace was worried her pulse was going to be racing all day, but the comfort of the familiar actions calmed her down. She did truly enjoy her work, she just would rather do it for herself and not at the end of a gun. Before she even had time to think about it, she saw the Grays coming with the seeds. It was time. She felt her pulse rising again.

She shook her head and took a deep, steadying breath. She said a silent prayer for strength as she reached for her trowel. She felt the handle hit her hand, but she missed grabbing a hold of it. The trowel fell off the table. She watched it fall as if in slow motion. The small shovel hit the ground with a loud clang. She hadn't even intended to drop it. As she was halfway down to picking it up, she remembered her plan to *pretend* to drop the shovel so she could get the seeds. And here she was having actually dropped it. A true accident she had been planning to fake.

It made her performance a lot more realistic as she bent down to grab the shovel. Once down, she fumbled the handle a little with her right hand. At the same time she slid her left hand under her dress. She closed her right hand on the shovel and her left on the packet at the same time and quickly stood, enclosing the packet entirely with her hand. She then turned and stood in the position of shame, waiting for the dismissal of the Gray. Her shovel was in one hand to be examined and her left hand was closed against her body. The packet felt like it was literally burning a hole in her hand.

After a moment, a Gray approached her. He didn't say anything as he surveyed her and the table behind her. After a moment he grunted and walked away. Grace curtseyed and then turned back to her table. Working quickly and praying she wouldn't be seen, she opened the packet, dumped the seeds into her hand, and shoved the packet into her mouth. It was the only place she could think to hide it. She continued praying as the Gray stopped at her station.

He pushed a cart in front of him with a small bucket full of seeds. Grace kept the seeds cupped in her hand as she grabbed a handful of seeds. She was careful not to drop any of her cucumber seeds in the bucket. She put the seeds into a smaller bowl next to the bucket before grabbing the bowl and turning back to her table. The paper in her mouth was softening around her tongue. The taste was awful but she worked hard to keep her face from showing anything.

A second cart followed behind. From this one Grace unloaded several plastic trays full of planters. When she was done, the cart moved on. Grace waited silently, mouth full of dissolving paper. She broke it into manageable pieces with her tongue and started swallowing what she could, working hard not to be noticed. She grimaced uncontrollably at the taste. Worried someone would notice her, she looked down at her desk for a distraction. Her eyes were drawn to the larger seeds that she was supposed to plant. She felt her heart rate rise again and closed her eyes.

Grace thought about what her and Rhys had been through the past few weeks. She felt a moment of awe at the power of God. Had He not intervened, Rhys would not have found those seeds and Grace probably would have been caught a moment ago. God was truly delivering them at this time, which meant He had something planned for them. Grace said a silent prayer of thank you as she finished swallowing the paper. She opened her eyes and glanced down the row. The Grays were handing supplies to the last workstation. Once everyone had what they needed, they would start working.

Grace looked down at the seeds she needed to plant. The seeds White Connors believed to be Nightshade but were actually cucumber. She took a deep breath, said one last prayer, and started working as soon as the soft bell rang out. She felt herself sliding into her normal rhythm. Her body moved smoothly through the actions, almost without her control. Grab a planter, dig a small hole, plant a seed, fill the hole, apply just the right amount of pressure, water, slide away and start the next. Her body relaxed in the comfortable motions. She wasn't even aware of which specific seeds she was planting. After about thirty minutes, she looked down and realized the cucumber seeds were gone.

Grace was shocked to see that she was done. She had been so wrapped up in her thoughts that she had almost absentmindedly planted all of the larger seeds. She'd actually planted most of her bowl already. She wouldn't even be able to pick out the planters she'd used for the larger seeds. They'd felt to her like any other seed. She smiled and prayed. She'd done her part. Now it was truly in God's hands. And God had even provided that, with a sudden and shocking chance to get out before she'd be caught. She felt herself relax and had to fight to keep herself from smiling for the rest of the day. Now she worried about bringing attention to herself for her giddiness when it had been for her anxiety just a few minutes ago.

The rest of the day passed without incident. She felt herself locking into her usual rhythm, but found more satisfaction out of it than usual. As the final bell rang she felt proud of the work she'd done that day. The plants she helped grow provided one of the only food sources within the complex. Most of what she grew went to the Whites, but she saw the occasional tomato or bean in the hands of some Grays. Knowing she was spreading a little light made her feel good about what she did.

She turned and waited to be escorted out of the building. When five minutes passed with no one moving, Grace realized something was different. They would rarely move a little slower but it was unheard of to be a full five minutes off schedule. Grace felt herself jump as the door to the Gardens banged opened. She looked up and saw White Connors enter the building. She spun her head forward and stood as still as possible.

Connors slowly walked through the door of the Garden, looking out over the room full of people. "Stay where you are please," Connors said. "I don't desire to be a burden to any of you. You have earned my blessing for the diligent work you so and I am feeling merciful today, so please remain as you are."

With that, he clapped his hands and began a slow circuit around the room. He made a show of looking at the posters along the wall. He felt in the soil of some plants, the leaves of others. He brought a few flowers to his nose for a smell. While he was doing this, the entire room was standing and waiting in silence. He finally walked up to Grace's table. He glanced to the newly filled planters on her desk. He stopped and stared. Grace glanced through her hair and saw a confused look on his face. Grace could do nothing but watch as his confusion turned to fear and then rage. He glared at Grace for a second before turning away.

Grace watched as he stormed to the central podium. He stared out over the room for a moment, watching the silent crowd. He raised his hands and snapped out, "For All Are One."

"And One Serves All," the room echoed back. Connors turned and left the room. Grays were looking at each other with confused faces, but the Colors remained staring forward. Grace watched out of the corner of her eye as Connors stopped at the door and spoke quietly to the Gray guarding the entrance. The guard looked over Connors's shoulder and made eye contact with Grace.

Grace tried to remain still, praying they didn't know she was watching them. She slowly dropped her head and turned away. She chided herself for being stupid enough to watch and bringing attention to herself. She jumped again when the door to the building slammed shut.

"Attention!" one of the Grays called out, voice echoing in the open room. "Follow." He turned and started walking quickly. The Colors, familiar with the daily routine, stepped into their positions quickly and quietly. Grace stepped into position, joining the line as they moved toward the door. Her heart was still racing and she couldn't stop it this time.

She knew it was coming but still cringed away from the Gray's hand. "Not you," he said sternly. His hand gripped her arm as he pulled Grace out of line. "Connors wants a word with you in his home." Grace nodded and stepped to the side quietly. She watched the rest of the women leave, trying to fight back the jealousy she felt. She thought about anyone else going through what she might be facing and felt her jealousy melt away. She decided that if anyone of them had to face Connors, she'd rather it be her. She felt she had a weapon against him, though she wasn't entirely sure what it was.

When the room had finally emptied, the Gray sighed. Grace remained quietly watchful, unsure how to act around the man. He confused her more when he held the door open for her. He kept his head down and held his arm out, gesturing that she should leave first. Grace had been expecting something much harsher and was confused by the gentleness. Once they were both through, the Gray turned and locked the door.

The man said, "Alright. That's that. Follow me, please." Grace was a still confused by his courtesy but followed close behind. She kept her eyes down as they walked the path she'd taken a month before toward the Tower.

She didn't feel quite as scared this time, but wasn't really sure why. When she remembered that they were leaving in a few days, it brought her calm. She just had to survive today. Whatever else he asked she could agree but wouldn't have to follow through. Within a few minutes, they were at the Tower.

Two guards that Grace hadn't seen before were at the gate. These were much less hostile than the first time she'd been here. Grace realized they must have been lower rank than the man guiding her because they both stood at attention when they saw his face. They remained at attention while the man ushered Grace through the gate and onto the white cobbles. He stayed behind; apparently she was going the rest of the way alone.

"Ah, wait!" he said to her. He put his hand on his face and glanced around. No one else was in sight and he relaxed slightly. He quickly reached around the corner and grabbed the blue booties. He gestured to Grace to come closer and put them on. Grace had a flash of how it might feel to refuse, but let it go. She quickly walked over to the guard and took the booties from him to cover feet. The older man relaxed once she was done. He nodded to Grace and then turned and left.

Grace turned and faced the Tower again. She slowly made her way along the white path. She felt like something terrible was going to happen, but it was a quiet, peaceful walk. She approached the door and was about to knock when she remembered the window on the side. She touched the screen and touched Connors's name. She watched as the screen went dark for a second then the face of Connors filled the window. He looked genuinely frightened.

"Oh, great. You're here. Come up." She jumped as a loud buzzing sound rang out from the door. She pulled on the metal handle to open the door. She walked down the hall and into the strange moving room again. It brought her up and opened to the angry and also panicked face of Connors.

"What did you do?" he asked loudly. "Did you plant them?"

"Yes, sir," Grace replied quietly. Her head exploded as his fist struck her. When the shock was over, Grace realized that it hadn't hurt as much as she'd thought. Her face stung and her head hurt a little, but it wasn't anywhere near the worst pain she'd had. She looked up at Connors. He was staring at her in shock. He looked at her, looked at his hand, then back at her.

"How did I hit you?!" he asked. "Y-you-yo," he stammered. "You must have wanted it. Yeah. That's it." As he spoke he gained more confidence. "You knew you screwed me over and you wanted to be hit. Because you deserve to be hit."

A silence filled the air before he continued, "Well?! What do you have to say for yourself?"

After a moment of silence, Grace pulled her shoulders back and met his eyes. A picture of Rhys filled her mind. She tried to imitate his posture. His strength. Connors shrank back as she stood tall. She felt powerful and realized that the man in front of her was not. He was weak, sickly, sniveling. He looked afraid of her. "You asked me to plant them, sir," she replied. "I did as I was told."

Connors shrank back from her gaze. He paced the floor in front of her. As he paced, he rubbed his nose, chewed on his fingernails,

and talked. Grace half listened to what he said but was more fasci-
nated by his behavior. He didn't stop moving. A white powder on his
nose stood out to Grace. The more she watched, the less intimidated
she was of him.

Grace listened to his rant, "But you planted them with a bunch
of others." He spoke quickly, barely taking time to breathe between
sentences. Grace couldn't tell if he even knew she was in the room
or if he was just talking to himself. "We aren't gonna be able to tell
which ones we want! And no way can I get rid of them without him
knowing. He's gonna know. Right away. And once it really starts
growing, he'll find it. And he'll find me. He'll know it was me. Then
what? I gotta stop it. But how? I don't know what to do!"

Grace was shocked to see tears forming in the man's eyes.
Connors finally seemed to remember she was there. He glared at her
and said, "I will not get killed cuz of you!" He stepped toward her.
Grace couldn't tell if he was getting ready to kill her or hit her again
or what he was doing.

"I can tell which is which, sir," she said quickly.

He stopped in his tracks meeting her gaze. He seemed to be
weighing if he could believe her or not. Trust her. He stopped moving and then gave her a small smile. "What?" he asked simply.

"In two weeks I should be able to tell which plant is which. I
can identify it for you when the first leaves poke through. Does that
help?" Connors stared at her as if unsure if he should believe her or
not.

After a moment he said, "How?"

"Well, sir," Grace replied, "I was raised a Gray. Raised in the
Gardens, and taught by my mother to care for plants since I was a
child. I can identify any plant in that Garden by its leaves the day it
sprouts."

Connors still looked skeptical, but appeared hopeful.
"Seriously?" Grace just nodded. "From those tiny first little leaves you
can tell what it's gonna be?" Grace nodded again. "No way. There is
absolutely no way that you can do that. No way can anyone do that."

Grace waited silently, not arguing but knowing that she could
do it. Connors looked at her for another minute then chuckled and

said, "Alright. Well if you can do it like you say, you might have just stayed your execution for another couple weeks at least. I brought you up here to have you killed. I wanted an answer first but that's it. If you can truly find me my plant, I'm willing to believe you. But you gotta prove it. I'll be coming to your Garden in two weeks and you will identify my plants for me."

Grace nodded and turned to leave. "Wait, you think that's it?" Connors voice rang out from behind her. "You almost give me a heart attack, almost get me killed, and think you're getting away from here with a warning?"

Grace turned back to Connors. She knew what he wanted and knew there was no way to fight or resist. She did the only thing she could think to do. As he put his hands on her, she declared, "I am under the protection of Jesus Christ."

He let out a slight shriek and jumped back at the name of Jesus Christ, like he'd been burned. It seemed something beyond his control because he gave her a very confused look. He regained his composure and became angry. Grace could see a hate-filled lust in his eyes. He stepped toward her again. As he moved he said, "That name has no power over me."

Grace felt herself quiver with fear for a moment. She felt his hands on her arms again as he started to move her. Strength she couldn't explain filled her body. She stood tall, shoulders back and declared loudly, "My body is under the protection of Jesus Christ. You have no power here."

Connors jumped back again. This time he fell to the ground. He looked up at her, startled and confused. He looked to his hands and his feet. Grace thought he might throw up as he looked back at her face. He stared for a moment before turning away, rolling onto his side.

Grace almost felt pity for the man. Then she remembered what he was about to do to her and the pity left. She stared down at the man, surprised to see that he was crying. She pushed the button on the wall, and stepped out of Connors's room. Her final view as the doors slid closed was of a sniveling, sobbing man crumpled on the floor.

CHAPTER 21

⌒⌒⌒

R hys felt his body freezing in terror. He stared at Wayne who stood just out of his reach. Rhys felt his heart lift seeing the smile on his friend's face again. Then his terror returned as he looked more closely at Wayne's face. Wayne stared at Rhys with a small, sad smile. He was waving at Rhys with one arm while his other was wrapped around his wife's shoulders. He stood looking at Rhys while a faceless man crept up behind. The shadowy man raised a rock in his hand.

Rhys tried to yell but his voice caught in his throat. He lifted his foot to step forward but found he couldn't move it. He looked down and saw he was standing in a pool of black slime, some of which seemed to be sticking to his ankle. His stomach filled with terror when he realized that it wasn't slime but fingers wrapped around him. As soon as he became aware of the fingers, a large, black figure materialized out of the goo behind him. He followed the fingers up a thick black arm, shoulder, neck, and finally arrived on the smiling face of a demon.

He had never seen a demon before and hadn't taken them too seriously. He figured they were real, but distant, like the ancient kings in a history book. He had the same feeling about the angels, actually. He read often in the Bible about the Heavenly Hosts, but thought of them more as something abstract. Certainly not something capable of grabbing his foot.

The demon snarled its sharp, pointed teeth at him. Rhys jumped in pain as the demon's talons dug into his skin. He reached down to pull the claws off his leg, when Wayne's voice cut across.

"It's OK, Rhys," Wayne said serenely.

Rhys felt his attention yanked back to the moment and off the demon. He remembered he needed to save Wayne. As he looked at the distance, though, he knew couldn't make it. But he didn't need to get to Wayne, he just had to speak and he could stop it. All he had to do was tell the truth, and Wayne would be saved. He stood tall and took a deep breath. As he did, he saw the face of his wife in the crowd. He stopped. In an instant, the demon clawed its way up Rhys's body. Rhys felt his mouth fill with foul, rotten flesh.

Rhys tasted the black mass and wanted to vomit, but his mouth was completely filled. He struggled to breathe while the demon slowly moved its face toward Rhys's. The pressure let up and Rhys was finally able to breathe again. He opened his eyes and realized there was no where he could look except into the black, hate-filled eyes of the demon perched on top of him like a vulture.

I'll show you what could have been, Rhys heard the voice fill his mind. The vision changed, and Rhys was pulled out of himself. He looked down and saw a glowing shadow of himself. He watched as that shadow stepped forward while raising a hand. Rhys saw light pouring out of his mouth, filling the ears of the crowd around him. The crowd's eyes lit up and then turned to face the man behind Wayne. The crowd took the rock and threw it to the ground, before raising a hand and pointing the man away.

When the man had left, the crowd turned to Rhys and stared, eyes still glowing. Rhys opened his mouth and spread more light, causing the eyes of a few others to brighten. Rhys then turned and led the large mass out, leaving a shrinking darkness behind. Rhys could just make out a large group of angry demons, similar to the one in front of his face. His vision leapt forward and he found himself pulled out of the eye of the demon and back into his body.

The demon moved and Rhys saw what had actually happened. The rock fell and Wayne's entire head caved in. Blood started pouring out of his eyes and ears. Rhys saw a short blast of light come from behind Wayne's eyes just as the rock fell. Rhys looked over and saw the same thing happen to Mary, including another brief flash of light.

Rhys turned away and realized the entire street was congealed with the black mass he stood in. He saw the faces of his family again, though this time contorted with pain. He saw demons reaching out of the blackness and latching onto them. As he continued turning, Rhys noticed that every person had a demon pulling them down. The sky was filled with darkness as demons swarmed the air around him. Some people were pulled so low they were crawling on the ground, feeding the demons a constant stream of darkness off of their bodies. A few individuals in the crowd stood taller.

The members of his family were some of those who stood. All those standing were reflecting a light between each other. That light broke through the darkness from above and poured into the souls of those standing. From there, the light reflected all around, driving the demons back. Rhys was proud to see Grace, Lily, and Thomas glowing with light and standing tall. He could see that the demons were still able to find shelter in their shadows, but his family wasn't pulled down like the others. The light seemed to hold the demons at bay. Rhys smiled as he realized he felt that same light pouring into him and being reflected out. The demon who was filling his mouth screamed out in pain and Rhys's nostrils were filled with the smell of something burning.

Rhys let out a sigh of relief as the demon rushed behind him, returning to his spot at Rhys's feet. Rhys pulled his boot up and felt a wave of revulsion at seeing the demon's fingers still wrapped around his boot. But his attention was pulled away from the demon and to the bright light filling him from above. He sensed a figure floating in front of him as his body filled with warmth. The light wrapped around him and his mind filled with peace and comfort. Rhys felt himself melting into the light. Melting into love and joy.

* * *

A bell rang out, waking Rhys from his dream. He was still filled with feelings of peace and joy, but they were fading quickly. He remembered that his friend had died and that he hadn't done anything to stop it. He felt himself filling with guilt again. It had been seven days and he couldn't seem to move past it. The guilt was building with each passing day and he knew that he needed to do something now.

Tonight, the family was planning on leaving. They had no choice and couldn't wait. After what Connors had said and done to Grace, she wouldn't have another chance. She was doing everything as normally as she could at work. But they both knew if she didn't deliver the "poison" to Connors in a week, he would have her killed. They couldn't wait another week and risk anything. It had to be tonight. And Rhys felt his body freezing with panic again.

The last time they had attempted to escape, Rhys had been fine. He had been able to lead them where they needed to go. Now, for some reason, his body wasn't behaving like it was supposed to. He was bumping into things, knocking things over. He nearly fell tripping over the ground yesterday. He knew if he didn't get himself in line, something would happen that would cause them to be caught. He couldn't risk it.

"Grace, I need to talk to you about something," Rhys said quietly. Grace was sitting on the edge of the bed. She looked over her shoulder, her smile fading as she saw the seriousness of his face.

"Of course," she replied. "What's going on?"

"I can't stop thinking about it. I'm even dreaming about it and I know if I don't figure something out I'm gonna mess up tonight and get us caught. I'm so sorry." Rhys said it all quickly, knowing he was doing a very poor job explaining himself. Grace's eyes filled with concern as she moved across the room. She sat next to him and put an arm around his shoulder.

"Slow down. We'll be fine tonight. You'll do fine tonight. I trust you and I know that you are an amazing man. Only you could save me. I love you and you are going to save me tonight." Grace pulled his head to her shoulder, running her hands through his hair as she whispered. She hoped what she said was reassuring. She wasn't quite sure what was bothering him specifically.

They sat like that for a moment, enjoying each other and the silence. When he was ready, Rhys took a deep breath and then sat up, facing Grace. Facing himself in her eyes and her response. "I could have saved him, Grace," Rhys said. "I could have saved him and I didn't. I let him die."

Grace stared at him in shock for a moment. This was not what she had expected. After a moment she shook her head, bringing herself back to her husband. "Rhys, that's not true. That's a lie. That's the devil talking. Number one, if God had wanted you to save him, you would have. But second, there is no way they would have let him live no matter what you might have done. Once they found that book, they were going to kill him. Kill everyone. We're lucky they didn't kill anyone else, actually."

Rhys looked at her, confused for a second. "No, Grace. No, if I would have just told them the book was mine. If I would have spoken up and told the truth, they would have spared him and killed me."

"What, you don't think he would have said something to save you? You think Wayne would have just sat there while you died?" Grace replied, quietly.

"Well, no, I suppose he wouldn't have." Rhys's face was shifting from pained to questioning.

"No he wouldn't have. He would have said it was found in his house so it was his and you were lying, trying to protect him or something." Rhys was watching her attentively, soaking up the words. "And anyway, as soon as you spoke up, the Grays would have been on you. They would have thrown you with him just for speaking. Then killed you both. And me. And the kids."

"But if I could have said something, maybe I could have convinced others to speak up," Rhys said. Grace saw a look of hope in his eyes.

"Maybe," Grace replied sadly. "Maybe one day enough will be that brave. But not yet. Honey, you remember that it was those same people who actually killed him, right?" Rhys looked surprised at the thought.

"Oh yeah," he said. "I kind of forget that part. To me, it seems like it was just that Gray you talked to. Jones?"

"Nope, he didn't lift a finger. Well not until he shot them anyways. He didn't have to. Our neighbors were more than willing to prove themselves not Christian. Willing to prove they were with the Grays and the Whites. But you're right, it wasn't everyone. I just don't think enough people didn't participate to overtake those who did. Again, not yet." Grace pulled his head back to her shoulder. She heard Lily and Thomas getting breakfast ready in the kitchen.

Rhys held his head against her shoulder for a moment longer before he said, "You really think they'll be ready some day?"

"If we can get enough of God's light out, I don't think anyone will be able to resist." Grace replied. "Now, we better get up and going. Don't want to be late for our last day, right?"

Rhys smiled at her and stood, extending a hand. She took it and felt herself swept to her feet with his strong pull. She still felt herself impressed by his strength at times. She smiled as he wrapped his arms around her, pulling her into a warm embrace. He held her like that, swaying back and forth and kissing the top of her head for a moment. She melted into the strong, hard muscles of his chest, a warmth filling her chest.

"You're amazing, you know that?" he said. She didn't reply but pushed gently back. She looked up at him and he gave her a gentle, loving kiss. "Thank you."

"I love you," she replied. "Feeling better about tonight?"

He realized that his tension had left him. He felt light for the first time all week. A weight and darkness had settled on his shoulders almost as soon as he was alone that first day after Wayne had been killed. He had been able to stay strong for his family, but when he left for work and was alone, the guilt set in. He only recognized it now that it was gone, but he'd been carrying that weight all week. And it was finally gone. He showed his wife a radiant smile in answer before he kissed her again. She chuckled and pinched his butt. He jumped back and she darted around him and out the room. Rhys followed with a smile.

CHAPTER 22

⸻ ❧ ⸻

Thomas knew he had to do it now. If he waited any longer, the rest of the class would be there and he would lose his chance. He reached into his pocket and pulled out the note he'd written. He'd been working on it all week, ever since Lily told him that she had invited a boy. Thomas hadn't even thought about it before, but realized that he couldn't leave without making sure Isaiah wouldn't worry and would know where he went.

He'd written the note in secret, afraid his father would make him destroy it if he found out. To Thomas, the thought of his only friend worrying about him made it worth the tiny risk of getting caught. Thomas had it all figured out so getting caught seemed so unlikely as to be irrelevant.

Thomas felt a wave of pride in how well he'd written the note. He was pretty sure he'd spelt all of the words right and his writing was very neat. He rubbed the note between his fingers as he entered the back of his classroom. He stepped forward and turned, seeing Isaiah in his usual seat, right next to Thomas. They'd been sitting next to each other all month and that was about all it took to be Thomas's best friend. That and their punishment together that first day.

Thomas took his seat. As he did, he dropped the note into Isaiah's hand. Thomas had his eye on the Gray in the front of the room, but the man looked bored. Isaiah held the note and looked curiously to Thomas. "Hide it," Thomas whispered out of the corner of his mouth. He bowed his head and waited quietly, the habit all of the Color students in their class had fallen into so as not to get into trouble when the Whites entered.

Thomas felt relief as he watched Isaiah quickly hide the note in his shoe and sit back upright. No one had seen. The Gray was still absently looking around the room and out the window, and the other Color students still had their heads down. Thomas smiled to himself and said a quick prayer to God, thanking Him for the chance to help his friend.

Soon after, when the room was filled and waiting in silence, Thomas followed his fellow Color students in dropping to the ground. The Whites slowly entered the room quietly. Thomas listened to their robes flutter and fall to stillness. Then the Grays took their seats quickly. When the room was again quiet, the voice of their White teacher filled the room, "For All Are One!"

"And One Serves All," the class echoed back. This too had developed into a normal morning ritual for the students and the teacher over the course of the last few weeks. It had evolved slowly from one action to the next, each group of students trying to convey the proper respect to the White, but none entirely sure the best way to do it. The Color students bowed in the back until after the call and response, Gray students stood at attention until the White students sat, and the White teacher began the morning call.

Sometimes the teacher seemed to relish the quiet and the power, making the Color students hold the uncomfortable position for minutes. One teacher spoke about the importance of the Colors learning their place, so she made them hold that pose for the entire morning.

Thomas relaxed into his chair, feeling his leg muscles finally soften. Sitting was much more comfortable and meant that today should be a pain free lesson. Any punishments the Color students had earned were always dealt out at the start of class. Thomas had been called forward several times over the past few weeks. Once for glancing at a White. Another time for not sitting up straight enough in his chair which indicated a lack of the proper respect. He'd even been punished for breathing too loudly because he was "trying to block the voice of a White."

"Today class we will continue our discussion about families. To review, we have covered the Grays and their communal system of living without sex. The men remain with the men and the women with the women. Sex is done as a group one night a week with all Grays of age. Any children conceived are raised the same way. Males and females separated. Parents are irrelevant.

"Then we have the Colors. Colors live in their own houses in small families. Colors are allowed one child without intervention. Any family that has two children are punished. Both the man and woman are sterilized and made to live together from that point forward. Prior to this event, families are encouraged to mix and spread.

"There are some Colors who continue the evil tradition known as a "nuclear family." This family arrangement, as we learned, is very weak. With only one father and one mother, the children are not exposed to a diversity of thoughts and ideas. The family is also susceptible to attack from rebel forces with so few adults in each house.

"Today we will learn of the superior living arrangement of the Whites. Being pure, the Whites are all able to live together in the Tower. Whites have risen above gender expression, so trying to separate between men and women would be pointless. Everyone loves everyone in the Tower and love is freely given and freely shown by all. Children are born on a schedule to replace any Whites who move beyond this realm.

"If a woman finds herself with child but there is no White to replace, the fetus is aborted. This honor is not afforded to the Grays or the Colors for obvious reasons. I know the Whites know what an abortion is, but the rest of you may not. There are several variations of the ritual…"

The White continued through one of the most painful lessons Thomas had ever heard. He listened as she described babies being cut to pieces while still inside their mother. Some mothers allowed the baby to grow for months before it was killed so as to harvest more and larger parts. Those pieces were then used empower the Whites through medicine and technology. He was constantly reminded of the child sacrifice performed by pagan people for the false gods in the Bible. The practices the White was teaching today seemed eerily similar to those ancient rituals.

* * *

Lily settled into her chair and felt her eyes drawn up to Craig's chair. Craig's empty chair. As soon as she realized what she was looking at, she quickly pulled her glance away. She tried to find anything else in the room to focus her attention on. She eventually settled on a small ribbon one of the Gray's had put in her hair. It was a light gray and pretty and just a shade away from clouds she'd seen in the sky which would be the same color as Craig's-

STOP IT! she thought to herself. She was trying really hard not to think of Craig. Or Wayne and Mary. Or Charles. It had been a very stressful week for her and so far she'd been able to control herself by shutting off the pain. She did everything she could not to think about it. She knew it was going to catch up to her at some point, but she needed to get past this week first. After this week she could think about Wayne's laugh, Mary's smile, playing blocks with Charles, Craig's lips agai-

ENOUGH! she shut her mind. Thankfully for her the White entered the room and commanded her attention. She remained in her chair, head bowed and hands in her lap. Her instructor preferred to waste no time on the Color's charades, as she called them. Lily had been surprised one morning a few weeks ago when the White had shouted at the Colors to return to their seats early. Half of the Colors hadn't even gotten into the position of worship, Lily being one of them. Lily had been just about to drop her head when the White's voice broke out over the room:

"No! No more! Not today, damn it. I'm not wasting another second on you Colors. Waiting for you to bow and then again for you to return to your chairs. I can see the hostility in your movements. Your bodies throw off constant micro-aggressions towards me and I can feel each and every one of them. No. I'm not going to do it anymore. From now on, when I arrive you will remain in your seats. You can assume whatever position you find properly subjugating. But, just know that if I detect any further micro-aggressions, they will be dealt with swiftly and without remorse. I have tolerated enough hatred. Enough anger from you. Endured enough pain."

Lily had remained on the ground throughout the White's speech, knowing that to move at that time would have resulted in punishment. As soon as she stopped talking, the Colors leapt to their seats. They remained sitting each morning since. Anytime the White was in the room, the Colors were sitting with heads bowed and hands in their laps.

"...has been transferred and will no longer be with us." The White stopped talking for a moment and Lily felt her heart rise at what she'd heard. Lily's mind had been wandering and she missed the first part of what the White had said. The word "transferred" echoed in her mind. Her eyes darted to Craig's empty chair and back down. Her mind was racing. She tried to think of a way to ask the White to repeat herself. As soon as the thought entered her mind, she knew it would be impossible. Luckily for her, she didn't have to ask because the White surveyed the room and continued.

"So, Dominic, you take Craig's seat since he will no longer be needing it." She pointed to the young Gray who sat behind Craig. That boy stood and stepped forward, filling Craig's seat and crushing Lily's heart. She couldn't stop it. Couldn't hold back the tears any longer. She stood up and rushed out the room as quickly as she could. She heard noise in the room but couldn't process it. The only thing in her head at the time was Craig's face.

She cried as she stumbled down the hallway, knocking into the walls on either side of her. Lily had a hard time seeing through the tears running down her face. She couldn't breathe. She crashed through the door and onto the empty alley.

The sunlight hit her face and she stopped in the cool air for a moment. Then she heard a door open on the street nearby. She closed the door behind herself and rushed down the alley, deeper into the Color district. She rounded the corner and put her back to the building. She stayed like that for a minute while keeping silent. She knew she was out of sight but it was soon apparent she wasn't being followed either. For someone to find her, they would have to climb the fence and walk down the alley. She was alone for at least a little while.

After a minute of silence, Lily felt comfortable enough to let herself cry again. She slid her back down the wall, dropping to the ground. She buried her face in her knees and felt the anguish washing over her. The words "he's gone" were playing on a loop in her head. An endless rotation of Wayne, Mary, Charles, and Craig swung in front of her eyes as Lily cried. With each face came a new memory of time spent with the person. The longer she cried, the brighter the memories came.

Lily was surprised to find herself laughing at the memory of Wayne falling when Lily was able to pull the chair out from under him. She felt the anguish on the edges but the laughter seemed to be keeping some of the pain at bay. This brought another memory to mind, of Mary pulling her into a hug when she learned Lily had been hit by a Gray that day. Lily felt her chest warm just remembering the warm feeling of Mary's arms around her.

Lily remembered more and more good memories, almost like they were washing the painful memories away. Trading jokes with Charles and hearing his laugh fill the room. Studying God's word with Wayne and Mary and earning the look of pride in their eyes when she asked a good question. That final hug they had as two whole families. Lily felt her arms hugging her knees in love and not in pain, trying to recreate that moment.

Then Charles's face filled her eyes again. His dead face. Blood had dried in a streak along his face and the color had drained out of his skin. His eye lids were drooping. His head was hanging. His mouth was slightly open. Lily felt nausea fill her gut as the pain came flooding back in. She tried to stop it, but couldn't. She was washed with anguish and pain again and felt herself sobbing deeply. The joy was gone from the world. The light was gone. Her light was out. Charles's face warped into Craig's in her mind. Craig's dead face.

No, that's not true, she thought to herself. Craig wasn't dead, just not here. Lily felt a small stirring in her chest. The anguish seemed to crest and stop moving forward. She thought of Craig's face again and felt the stirring grow. The more that stirring grew, the farther the anguish fell back. Lily found her mind wandering to Craig's lips on hers and she felt herself smiling. She thought of the drawing he gave her. Or tried to. She was so glad to have seen the beauty he was capable of.

She thought of the last words she heard him say, "I love you, too." Lily felt the pain in her chest shift completely. It seemed to warp from anguish to longing. Hopeless to hopeful. Dark, empty pain to light, full pain. *He loves me,* she thought. And he's alive. And he's out there. And I'm going out tonight. She sat alone, her back pressed to brick wall of the school building. Her mind filled with possibilities of life and love and marriage and babies. An entire existence with Craig that might now be possible. Her mind filled with so many different fantasies she had a hard time keeping track of them all. And she let it wander as far as it could.

She almost jumped when the first Color walked in front of her. She realized the school day was done. She stood up and brushed off her pants. She peeked around the corner and watched for her brother. The Gray was paying more attention than normal to the class, but didn't seem to notice her. Thomas eventually stepped into the alley.

"Why are you hiding around the corner?" he asked when he got close enough that she'd be able to hear his whisper.

"I'll tell you later," Lily said with a smile. She took his hand and started walking home. "Let's get going. We've got a big night tonight."

CHAPTER 23

"Is it time yet, dad?" Thomas asked for at least the fifteenth time. Everyone was more on edge tonight than they had been last week. Rhys figured it was due to the death of Wayne, Mary, and Charles. Things felt a lot more serious now. The stakes were higher tonight. If they didn't get out, they'd be killed. There was no staying here and no going back. It was now or never.

"Not yet, bud," Rhys replied with a smile. He knew he needed to be strong for them. They needed him to lead them now or he was going to lose them all. "Tell you what," he continued, "why don't we pray about it?"

Grace and Lily both looked relieved. They had been pacing through the living room and the kitchen nonstop for a while now. They smiled and walked over to Rhys, holding out their hands. Rhys took his wife's hand and held out his hand for Thomas. Thomas smiled and nodded to his dad. Rhys felt a surprising wave of pride seeing approval in his twelve year old son's eyes. All Rhys could do was smile back.

"Can I start?" Thomas asked. Rhys was somewhat taken aback but nodded. Thomas didn't usually volunteer to lead in prayer. "Our father, Who art in Heaven, hallowed be Thy name," Thomas began. He wasn't quite whispering, but wasn't talking either. The family could hear him well, but his voice wouldn't carry out of the room.

"Amen," the family finished. They all opened their eyes and looked at each other. They smiled amongst themselves and were about to continue in prayer when a voice broke through their silence.

"Well, what do we have here?" They all jumped and turned toward the window. A strange man's face filled the open window. Rhys felt his blood run cold when he saw the gray uniform. Rhys realized with a shock they had just prayed in front of an open window. Might as well have done it in the middle of the street. Rhys could only stare in shock, unable to make his mouth move to answer. He did the only thing he could think of and bowed his head.

The man chuckled to himself and then let himself into their shack. Rhys used his arm to guide the rest of the family behind him, guiding them back into the kitchen. No one made a sound as the Gray shut the door then turned to face Rhys from across the room. The Gray then pulled out his weapon and pointed it at the ground.

"You know what I could do to you right? To all of you?" the man said. He shook his head and smiled at them. Rhys could see the excitement in his eyes. And the malice. "Thank the Whites! I never thought I'd see a day like this. I don't even know what do to."

Rhys heard the pitch rising in the man's voice as he got more excited. Rhys noted for the first time just how young the man was. He was barely a boy really and looked younger by the minute. Rhys imagined the scenarios that must be running through the boy's mind. Call another Gray and turn them in for a reward. Call a White for a public execution. Shoot them on the spot himself. Rhys felt terror rising in his chest as the boy's face warped to something dangerous. The boy looked over Rhys's shoulder at his wife and daughter.

"You," the boy said, pointing to Lily. "I came here to see you in the first place. After that fit you threw in class, I knew something was up. But when a Color student handed me this," he held up a small, folded piece of paper. Thomas let out a small yelp of recognition. The Gray chuckled to himself and nodded, "I thought it might be yours," he said smugly. "And I just knew that I had to come see to this personally."

"I came looking for a few answers. Maybe rough you up a bit. But the Whites have truly blessed me today. Now, how to take advantage of such a blessing? Any suggestions?" The boy was really enjoying himself now. He was swaggering around the room, keeping the gun trained on Rhys the entire time. Rhys kept a protective arm in front of his family. Rhys noticed Grace had her arms wrapped around the children, hugging them into her body. She turned to start moving deeper into the kitchen and away from the gun.

"No, no, no," the boy said as soon as Grace started moving. "No, no. None of that. You'll all stay here, I think."

Grace stopped and turned to face the boy again. Tension hung in the room as Rhys and Grace were waiting for the boy to make a move. The boy was waiting too, though he didn't seem to be sure what he was waiting for. The room filled with silence. The boy's face grew more uncomfortable with each passing second. Finally, he broke the silence, stepping toward Rhys.

"Enough of this," he said. "Quit standing there and get down on your knees." Rhys prayed for guidance as he followed. As he prayed, he felt comfort and peace. He stepped forward, trying to keep the Gray as far away from his family as possible. As Rhys started to bow he noted that he was less than an arm's length from the boy's out-stretched arm. Rhys took a deep breath, praying silently to God. Then he leapt into action.

He slammed his arm forward, hitting the gun in the boy's hand. He pushed the hand away from his family and toward the room. The look of shock on the boy's face was almost comical. Rhys took one more step and chopped the side of his hand into the young man's neck, striking with as much force as he could.

The boy dropped the gun and then dropped to his knees. His hands shot to his neck. Rhys quickly ran over and grabbed the gun, pointing it at the Gray kneeling in front of him. Rhys stood for a moment in shock at the feeling of the gun in his hand. He'd never fired one but it felt natural in his hand and, by design of the gun, he knew exactly what to do.

The boy seemed to be trying to talk, or maybe yell, but he wasn't able to make any noise. "Stop that," Rhys said firmly. The boy stopped immediately. "Move. Go to the kitchen," Rhys said quickly. He gestured with the gun. The boy stared up at him in shock, tears filling his eyes. He started shaking his head. Rhys felt a wave of pity fill his chest at the desperation and terror he saw.

"I'm not going to hurt you," Rhys said quietly. "I just need you to get away from the window. Now! Go! Please," he added more gently.

The boy dropped to his hands and started crawling along the floor. Rhys could hear him sniveling and saw a trail of tears and slimy snot on the floor behind the boy. Rhys was a little surprised at the level of disgust on his daughter's face.

Eventually the boy arrived at the kitchen. Once there he dropped to the floor and lay on his side, hugging his knees to his chest. He rocked slowly back and forth, quietly sobbing to himself. His body seemed to be convulsing.

Rhys looked up and met Grace's equally flabbergasted face. She had a twinkle of humor in her eye that almost made Rhys smile for a second. Then he remembered how serious this situation was. He had just attacked a Gray. They were going to kill him. Tonight. As soon as this boy realized that all he has to do is yell out, Rhys would be caught and killed. The gun only had a few bullets, so he couldn't kill everyone. He'd never be able to fight his way out.

He turned to Thomas and said, "Go get some clothes." Thomas nodded and ran down the hall. He looked to Lily and said, "You too. Anything you've got. We need it all." Grace met his gaze with a confused look in her eye. "Do you have your sewing basket?" Rhys asked. Grace nodded and stepped into the living room. Rhys was alone with the young man waiting for his family to return. He said one more prayer for strength and protection tonight of all nights. He felt the usual comfort and peace wash over him with the prayer and the remembrance that God was in control. He opened his eyes as Thomas returned to the kitchen followed by Grace and Lily.

Rhys took the basket from Grace's hand and exchanged it for the gun. Grace pointed the gun at the young boy, but watched Rhys as he took her scissors out of the basket. Then he began cutting the clothing into strips, working silently and quickly. Once he had two pieces, he tied them together. Grace nodded and turned her attention back to the boy. Lily still looked confused so Rhys handed her the two, tied-together strips, and then cut a third. He handed her the third strip and she got it. She quickly tied that to the first.

After a few minutes, they had a rope of clothing that was a few feet long. A few minutes later, they didn't have enough room to keep it straight anymore. Rhys nodded to himself and then stepped toward the boy. Rhys grabbed the boy's shoulders and lifted him to a sitting position.

The boy looked confused, through the tears and snot on his face. He was still holding his neck and Rhys realized he'd been trying to yell out for a while now. He was still not able to yell. Rhys felt relief as he took one end of the rope and filled the boy's mouth with it. The boy stopped trying to yell out and started trying to spit out the wad of cloth, breathing deeply and quickly through his nose.

Rhys worked quickly, wrapping the cloth around the boy's head to hold the wad in his mouth. Then he wrapped the boy's arms, hands, and down his legs to his feet. The boy was left hog-tied with his face pressed against the ground. The clothing was wrapped as tight as Rhys could get it. He was reasonably sure that the boy wouldn't be able to escape, but could still breathe. The ropes might hurt, especially if he struggled, but shouldn't cause any serious cuts. He couldn't be sure but had to take the risk. He didn't want to kill anyone, but wanted him tied up until he was found by someone else. Hopefully tomorrow morning.

Rhys secured the end of the rope with a final knot and stood. His entire family stared down at the boy for a moment. The boy looked over his shoulder, up at them. He'd stopped squirming and seemed to be waiting for them to move. The boy's attention was riveted on Rhys.

"I am going to get a Gray to tell him what you did to us," Rhys said. "You raped my wife and were about to rape my daughter when I was able to overpower you. How disgusting will you look in his eyes? Stay here, stay still, stay silent until I get back or Grace here will shoot you. Do you understand?" The boy nodded quickly. He looked sincere in his fear at least. Rhys hated lying but felt justified if it kept the boy quiet long enough to allow his family to escape.

"Good," Rhys nodded. He ushered his family out of the kitchen, through the living room, and out the front door. They walked quickly and quietly, darting between shadows as they had just one week prior.

Guess we are going to the gate early tonight, Rhys thought to himself. The gun in his hand at least gave him some confidence.

They took the same route through the city, avoiding main streets and lights whenever possible. As they moved, Rhys realized things felt so much different with a gun. The previous week, he'd felt helpless. Like a small rabbit. He knew that he would not be able to fight at all if caught. He would be at the mercy of anyone he came across.

But this week, with the gun in his hand, he felt like a hunter. A protector. He knew that he'd likely only get his family killed if he started shooting, but they'd be killed no matter what if caught. If they were shot, he would be saving them untold tortures. A quick death with each other, vs drawn out deaths alone. Going out in a gun fight sounded much more appealing to him the more that he thought about it. And the more grateful he was for the gun.

Luckily he didn't have to use it. They made it to the same house, looking out on the same gate. It was much earlier though, so Rhys gestured that Grace and the kids should sit down. He peeked out the window and saw a single Gray guard sitting at the gate. Rhys realized right then that there was only one thing standing in his way. He could get out. He could get his family out. The only thing stopping him was one man. And Rhys had a gun.

Rhys looked down at the gun and up at Grace. She had a look of concern on her face. Rhys looked back down at his gun. Rhys could tell she was worried and he knew why. She thought he might shoot the guard. Grace would never look at him the same if he killed someone. With that realization, the thought washed out from him. He shook his head and then settled in, putting the gun on the ground nearby. Grace relaxed once Rhys took his hand off the gun. She settled in with an arm around each of her children. No one slept. Rhys found a comfortable position where he could still see the guard. He waited for the man to move from his post so they could go.

A long time passed. Rhys thought 1:00 AM must be getting close, but he truly had no idea. A change of guard came and a new Gray stepped into the post. That was the only excitement for the entire night. Until the alarms started.

Rhys almost jumped when the blaring siren rang out. Lights burst on in the streets and Rhys dropped down. He watched as a patrol of Grays jogged along the wall. They stood at attention in front of the Gray guarding the gate. He saluted them and then the two men continued jogging along the exterior. The young man was alone and standing at attention. The lights remained on and the siren continued droning. Rhys was panicked.

He knew the guard would never leave his post now. Their chance was blown. He felt anxiety rising in his chest. He looked over his family. They looked back with terror in their eyes. They needed him to do something. They all knew what was at stake. There was no going back. Rhys steadied himself as he met Grace's eyes and nodded.

Rhys turned and looked back to the gate. The guard was still alone, but Rhys knew that couldn't last long. For now Rhys couldn't see anyone or anything else. He took a deep steadying breath and then made his way out of the building into the lit street. The Gray saw him immediately and pointed his gun at him. Rhys pointed his gun back. He saw the Gray's eyes fill with fear. They stared at each other, neither wanting the fire first, but neither wanting to back down.

"Private Gates?" Grace's voice called out over Rhys's shoulder. The guard looked stunned as Grace stepped out into the street. "Private Gates, is that you?"

"Yes," he replied simply. His entire demeanor had changed. The gun was shaking in his arms as Grace slowly stepped in front of Rhys. Rhys hated her being out front, but trusted her. As she passed Rhys she had met his eyes. He saw a plan in those eyes. He saw confidence. He dropped his gun.

As soon as Rhys's gun was down, Private Gates dropped his gun as well. Grace walked forward slowly, her arms in the air. "Of course it would be you," the guard said as Grace got closer. "I should have known." He sighed and looked around down the street. Then he looked back at Grace and smiled. "And to think, I almost shot your man."

"Well, thank you for not doing that," Grace stammered. An awkward silence filled the air.

"You know you can't stay here," Private Gates said, breaking the silence. "They found that Gray in your house. And I don't know what you got going on with Connors but that can't end well. I owe you my life for saving me. Consider us even." Grace's eyes filled with tears as the man talked. He stepped aside and turned his back on the gate. Rhys stepped out in front of Grace and rushed forward. The gate swung open freely and Rhys held it while each of his family members ran through. When they were all through he turned to the guard. They stared at each other for a moment.

"Thank you," Rhys said. It was all he could think to say, but he meant it. The Gray nodded in response. Rhys did the sign of the cross and said, "May God protect you and open your eyes." The man looked confused for a moment but then seemed to shrug it off. Rhys turned and stepped through the door, out of the city, and into darkness.

A darkness full of possibilities. Full of hope, of light, of love. He grabbed his wife's hand, put his arms around his children's shoulders and took his first steps into freedom.

CHAPTER 24

R hys looked out into the dark night and realized he had no idea
where to go. An open expanse lit softly by moonlight greeted
him. His family stood frozen around him. He looked out, trying
to make out any signs of movement. Any indication of where the
stranger might meet him. He truly considered the fact that the man
may be dead. The Grays definitely had his necklace. Rhys accepted it
as a very real possibility that there would be no one waiting for him.
He was alone and he was now solely responsible for his family's safety.

He still didn't know where to go but now he knew what he
needed to do. He needed to get everyone as far away from the
Complex as quickly as possible. He prayed as he leapt into action.
He hunkered down and rushed his family forward, looking for any
cover. The Grays had removed most of the buildings immediately
surrounding the gates, leaving an open field between the Complex
and any shelter. There were search lights roving through the debris at
odd intervals. Rhys breathed a sigh of relief as he looked to his right.
All of the search lights seemed to be shining on a forest to his right,
far away from where they were running. The Grays seemed to be
searching for them but were looking in the wrong spot.

Rhys kept an eye on the search lights as they made their way
carefully forward. Rhys prayed hard while they rushed through the
wasteland. They stopped at the first semi intact building they came
to for shelter. They crouched together in the darkness, each trying to
catch their breath. Before they did anything else, Rhys pulled them
all into a bowed circle, heads pressed together and arms around each
other's shoulders. "Thank You God," Rhys said. "Thank You for

Your protection, for leading us here, and for helping us to all get out together."

They separated and all wiped tears out of their eyes. Rhys took a moment to survey the room they were in. It had been gutted long ago, and half the building had collapsed. They had gotten in through a hole in the side of the building, and couldn't go any further into the building. They were safe for now but definitely couldn't stay.

Rhys motioned for his family to stay as he moved back to the hole. He glanced back to the Complex and was relieved to see darkness. No search lights. No activity. Nothing that he could see. He could hear a distant sound of yelling, but it sounded far from where they were. Looking the other way, his eyes followed a road cutting between the buildings around him and into the darkness. It seemed like the only way for them to go but Rhys wasn't sure. He didn't want to lead his family into further danger.

Rhys stepped away from wall and back to his family. They all crouched down and looked at each other in silence. They had mostly caught their breath and were just waiting to be told what to do next. Rhys could read a look of expectation in their eyes as they looked to him. He prayed their faith in him was justified.

Rhys met Grace's eyes and gestured to the road. "We follow that," he said quietly. "But try not to be seen. We don't know who might be out here and I don't want to be grabbed by someone bad. We'll watch for the man I saw and pray he'll be here to help us. But it is possible we're on our own."

Each of his family members met his gaze with serious expressions. He was surprised to see his gaze met with looks of excitement in the eyes of his children. He was proud of their bravery. He smiled to his wife, took her by the hand, and stepped out onto the road.

As soon as they started moving, they were blinded by a small, bright light to their side. "It's you!" a voice Rhys recognized called out. Rhys was shocked to see Samuel step into the light. The old man was cleaner than Rhys had ever seen him. The man also walked with a vigor Rhys found surprising. It was almost like meeting a new man. Samuel grabbed Rhys by the shoulders and pulled him into a hug.

Rhys was stunned by Samuel's strength. Rhys felt a warm, wetness through his shirt.

"Oh, thanks be to God," a new voice called out from behind Samuel. "I was really praying that I'd see you again." The stranger from the forest stepped forward, extending a hand toward Rhys. Rhys took his hand from around Samuel's embrace. Rhys's brain started to catch up. The shock of emotional change from fear to safety was difficult for him to process. The only thing he could think to do was gesture his family forward.

"This is my wife, Grace, and children, Thomas and Lily," Rhys said. At his words, Samuel opened his arms and pulled the whole family into one big hug. He wasn't making much noise, but didn't seem to be trying to be silent either. The stranger released Rhys's hand and stood back, smiling at Samuel's enthusiasm.

"It is an honor to meet you all, my name is Zack," the stranger said. He waved his hand with a flourish and bowed down to them. Thomas and Lily let out soft chuckles, but still seemed unsure of what was happening. Rhys noticed they each were watching the surrounding shadows with uneasiness.

"Well Zack, can you take us out of here?" Rhys asked. Samuel let out a bark of a laugh and stepped back, wiping tears from his eyes.

"I'm sorry," Samuel said, "I'm just so relieved to see you here. The Lord truly does answer prayers, doesn't He?"

"Yes He does," Zack replied with a smile. "But you're right we should get moving. You are the only refugees I've been able to reach. I am so glad you made it out, and it looks like barely..." Zack gestured to the Complex and the search lights sweeping over the trees.

Rhys felt his stomach drop slightly. "Yeah, that might have been my fault," he replied. "We sort of attacked and tied up a Gray on our way out. I'm thinking they must have found him."

Zack looked at them with shock then burst out laughing. "Well that's a story I'd love to hear!" he said. He put his arm around Rhys's shoulders and started walking. Rhys told him the story as he was escorted down the street, being led by the bright lights Zack and Samuel held in their hands.

After a couple of blocks, Thomas interjected, "I'm sorry, but what are those things you're holding? I've never seen anything like them." Rhys was glad his son had asked because he had been wondering the same thing.

"Oh, right," Zack began. "I suppose you haven't seen one, have you?" He held the item out for Thomas to take. Thomas grabbed it from his outstretched hand, looking at the strange item. He held it up to his face and winced back in pain. As he was moving, Zack had been saying: "just don't—Ope. Sorry I should have warned you sooner. Anyways, that is a flashlight. It is a portable light source we use."

Thomas had started waving it around, shining the light onto the crumbling buildings around them. "Cool!" he said. Rhys noticed that Thomas's voice was getting louder as they walked on. "Just like in the Bible!"

"What?" Zack replied. "I've read the Bible and I can assure you there is not a single mention of flashlights in the entire book. Unless we're reading different books."

"Yuh huh, there is" Thomas replied quickly, sounding very sure of himself. He had stopped moving and looked defiantly back at Zack. Thomas met Zack's gaze and stood his ground firmly. The whole group stopped moving for a moment, caught up in the conversation.

"In the Bible? The Holy Bible?" Zack replied. Thomas nodded once, definitively. Zack looked at Thomas then up at Grace and Rhys, and said with a smile, "Does he always give you attitude like this?"

"Just when he's sure of himself. But I'm with you, I've never read about flashlights in the Bible," Rhys replied.

"Alright, smarty pants," Zack said with a smile. "Let's hear it. What verse of the Bible talks about a flashlight?" Rhys could tell he still doubted, but Zack seemed curious to hear the boy out.

"Psalm 119: 'Thy Word is a lamp unto my feet and a light unto my path.'" Thomas replied. "If that doesn't sound like one of these flashlight thingies, I don't know what does."

Zack stared back at him, stunned for a moment before letting out burst of laughter. "Wow, you got me. That's it," he replied through his laugh. He put a hand on Thomas's shoulder as he took the flashlight back. He kept the hand on his shoulder as they walked forward. "You'll have to tell me what I owe you when we get to town," Zack said. Rhys followed close behind. Thomas looked back to his dad, smiling with pride and joy.

They continued walking for a few blocks, chatting with Zack and Samuel. They both seemed so at ease, Rhys felt his worry sliding away. He still had a hard time letting go of the fear of getting caught, but their attitudes helped him relax. He didn't know Samuel well, but he trusted him. And the other man seemed trustworthy as well. His willing discussion of Christ really put Rhys's mind at ease. As he thought about it, though, he realized he didn't really have an alternative choice but to trust.

They stepped up to something kind of like the large vehicles Rhys helped unload. This was a lot smaller, but had a similar shape. The door slid open and Rhys was surprised to see two rows of benches inside. Rhys stopped and looked questioningly at Zack, who stood with his hand on the open door.

"This is a van," Zack explained. "It is a vehicle we can use to drive you to a safe location." He stopped talking and was shining his light on the gun in Rhys's waistband. He smiled at Rhys and continued, "Well that's a surprise. Didn't think you'd come out armed but that's great! Do you know how to shoot?" he asked.

Rhys met the man's eyes and shook his head. "I thought not. Well, where I live, everyone has to take a basic firearm safety class. Since you already have a gun, I can give you a quick crash course just so you know a little of what you're doing. Safer for everyone. Later on, when we are further away, we can stop and fire off a few rounds if you want? Then you'll really get a feel for how it works and how to respect it."

Rhys nodded and watched carefully as Zack pulled out a gun of his own. Using Zack's gun and motions as a guide, Rhys quickly learned how to chamber a round, basic instructions on aiming, and how to eject and reload the magazine. He was far from proficient, but felt much more comfortable with the weapon. Grace, Thomas, and Lily watched the lesson, but didn't handle the gun themselves. Zack was an excellent and efficient teacher.

Ten minutes later Rhys put the safety on and slid the gun back into his belt. "Thanks," he said. He realized that he fully trusted Zack now. Why would Zack teach him to use the very thing that he might need for defense. He smiled warmly and shook Zack's hand.

"No problem," Zack replied. "It's actually a law where I live that every family own at least one firearm. And every member of that family needs to pass a proficiency test on the proper use of that firearm. Most people have their own on them at all times since the war, but we'll get to all that later. For now, we load up here and we'll drive you to the resettlement camp."

"Resettlement camp?" Rhys asked. He had so many questions, but couldn't ask them all. That was the first that came to mind, probably because it was the easiest.

"Yes, don't worry," Zack said calmly. "I know you have a million questions. My group put together a thing for me to read while we drive that will get you caught up. Not on everything but enough to get you started. It'll answer your most broad questions and then we can get into the details."

Rhys was still trying to keep up. His family looked just as lost as him. They stood at the entrance to the van and stared at each other. Rhys wasn't sure what to do so he did the only thing he could think of. He grabbed Grace's hand, closed his eyes, and prayed the Our Father. Within the first few words, the voices of every person in the group joined him. Rhys opened his eyes and watched Zack praying with him. It felt as if God had sent Zack directly to help them.

When the prayer was done, Rhys nodded to Zack and climbed into the van. He awkwardly shuffled over in the middle seat, deciding the let the kids scramble their way into the back. He didn't know if he'd even be able to fit back there, but he also wanted to keep himself between the older men and his kids. He trusted the men, but still felt a pull to protect his children. When they were all in the van, Zack smiled and closed the door. Then he climbed in the front and sat next to Samuel, who was already sitting in the front left seat.

"Alright, let's get going," Zack said. Samuel nodded and then moved something in front of him. Rhys jumped as the van roared to life. Samuel smiled at him with amusement in his eyes. "Don't worry, it won't bite." The van started rolling, lights shining brightly on the road in front of them. Rhys watched the crumbling houses speed past them. After a few minutes the crumble turned into burnt wreckages. Rhys had never been this far out and was surprised to see so much destruction. Holes were blown into the sides of buildings and almost every building was marked by fire. There were also several burnt vehicles along the road.

"What happened here?" Rhys asked.

"The Coup," Zack replied. "Tell you what, I'll answer all of your questions, but do you think you can just listen for a while? There's a lot to go through, and I promise we will answer everything, but it will go faster if I can catch you up to date first." Rhys nodded and Zack relaxed. He smiled reassuringly and then began reading.

Rhys and his family listened carefully and attentively as Zack began, "OK, well first off, everything you've been taught about our history is a lie."

CHAPTER 25

—— ⚬ ——

Z ack read, "You are currently living in what was used to be called the United States of America. There were once fifty states, joined together in union under one constitution to live together in peace. The states were supposed to be sovereign places, each able to decide their own laws and methods of living. An overarching federal government was supposed to be small and only necessary for military and to mediate issues between states. Unfortunately that federal government grew large and became corrupted.

"More and more commands were coming down, removing power from the states and centralizing it with the federal government. Laws were passed nationwide and expected to apply to everyone instead of only those who chose to live in that state. This meant that if you disagreed with a law, there was nowhere else to go.

"Federal taxes were drastically increased to help fund massive, unwieldy, beurocratic programs. These programs were very prone to corruption and allowed those in power to enrich themselves through back room deals. Taxes were collected federally to fund programs in a few areas scattered around the country, instead of state by state to fund programs locally. This funneled more and more money and power to elite, urban, highly populated cities and away from sparsely populated areas.

"The programs in these dense cities lured people, who brought more votes. Those in power then encouraged more programs to entice more people and the cycle continued. Those in the rural areas were generally fine providing for themselves. Unemployment in the sparsely populated areas was low and there was a general sense of: *you do your thing and leave me alone to do mine.* As these divisions continued, a physical separation was reinforcing the social separation.

"The elites worked to maintain their power through a façade called political parties. They divided the country into two by focusing on a few key issues. They pumped all of their power into these issues, drawing the attention of the people onto each other and away from the elites in charge. And it worked. The elites were able to divide the country into two, white skin or colored skin, gay or straight, man or woman, and, most powerfully, group or individual. Once these issues were discovered, they were able to keep themselves in power through social manipulation.

"Two factions were formed by the elite in what was supposed to be a United States. One faction, the Democrats, centralized in bigger cities and wanted a bigger government to help them. The second faction, called Republicans, was spread out through the rest of the US and wanted a smaller government to leave them alone. When the time was right, the elites put a plan into motion that would ensure they were kept in power. You have lived through the repercussions of that plan. For you to fully understand their plan, however, you first need to know a few other things about the world before the Coup.

"The elites controlled not just the cities, but also had a monopoly on what people could read or write. They used this power to twist the minds of any that they could. What was called the "Mainstream Media" pumped out stories designed to drive a wedge between these two factions. People were pitted against each other for their skin color, religion, sex, gender. Any difference that divided would be used and exploited. The elites spewed out stories of hatred and anger, especially if it could drive forward a narrative.

"The Mainstream Media focused attention on victims with the primary goal of group inclusion. People were encouraged to find ways to be victims and blame others for their problems. In general, people willing to do this happened to be Democrats while the people who took responsibility for their own problems tended to be Republicans. The elites used their media power to feed into the victim mindset of the Democrats and encouraged their anger and rage, blaming everything on the Republicans.

"While the Mainstream Media was doing that, Democrats in public schools were teaching children to hate. White students were taught that they were ancestors to oppressors and they should be ashamed. Taught that no matter what they did or said, they were already racist because of their ancestors. Black students were taught that they were the victims of white oppression at all times and they would never be able to rise above it. The only answer was to watch for the continued oppression so they could bring attention to it right away. This started a mindset in children to watch for the worst in others instead of the best. A mindset they carried into adulthood.

"Students were taught to disobey their parents and tear down the current authority. The students were told they were good and special and perfect the way they were. If their parents disagreed and wanted the students to be better, those parents were being hateful. The kids didn't need to change, society needed to change. And anyone who disagreed was a part of the system that was holding the students down.

"So, the media was pumping out hate, the schools were teaching division. They also attacked the men. Not any men in particular but the idea of 'man' was fought. Masculine traits were attacked as aggressive. Unless done by a female, then it was powerful. Female figures in television, movies, commercials, books, everything began overpowering the men around them. On every channel, through every escape, men were belittled, mocked, and emasculated.

"Some men fought this, particularly the Republican men, but the Democrat's control of media was so all encompassing that it became almost impossible for a Republican man to speak out. At this time, what is called the 'internet' allowed every person throughout the entire globe to speak instantaneously. Even this was also almost exclusively under the control of the elites. They used all of their platforms to spread their messages.

"When the time was right, they attacked on several fronts. A virus was released that spread throughout the populace. The media spread fear and panic throughout the country, claiming this virus to be "new" and "deadly." The only way to fight was to isolate from everyone and be alone. For over a year this went on. The cities, where people were already more willing to follow the government and more likely to be alone, isolated the entire time.

"The rural areas however were less compliant. Half of the time this was because they were simply unaware. People in smaller towns tended to be stronger and more resilient to social trends. They were already unlikely to follow authoritarian directives from a federal government that had grown too large in their opinion. The media wrote stories about small town, conservative, Republican people who weren't obeying the governmental edicts to cast blame on them. Stories written with the intent of stoking anger, jealousy, and envy in the large city, urban Democrats. And it worked.

"At the same time as the virus, a race war was started. Several stories were highlighted where a white officer killed a black victim. The facts of these stories were irrelevant, all that mattered was the white police officer killed an unarmed black person. All of the media covered the same stories 24/7. There was no escape and it did not matter where you lived. All media in all places covered the same, racially charged content. And all of the "reporters" were reading the same opinion.

"Groups of isolated, fearful, mis-educated, unappreciative, immature children who had been pent up for the past few months gathered in the streets throughout the large cities. These are the students who had been taught all their lives to look for ways to be victimized. Trained to watch the behavior of those they've been taught to hate for oppression. Once they took to the streets and started demanding "justice," there was no going back.

"Eventually, the gatherings in the streets became rioting. The anger filling these children was directed at anything that reminded them of their oppressors. Figures of authority like police officers or government buildings were most often targeted. It didn't take long for the police to stop working, at least in the big cities. The rioting didn't spread to the rural areas, but remained isolated in the bigger cities.

"While this was going on, there was a separate battle on the Christian faith. The elites seemed to understand that Christians were one of their strongest ideological opponents. There had been attempts to undermine the Christian faith for decades, but nothing had really stuck. People continued to be strong Christians despite making advancements in other areas. The elites had struggled, but finally found a powerful point of division within the church. Homosexuality.

"Churches were driven apart from within by emphasizing and normalizing homosexuality. It was pushed very strongly through all media in an attempt to corrupt as many as possible. This was found to be especially effective on children. Within a few years, half of all children and young adults were identifying as what they called LGBT.

"Many of these youths weren't part of the churches, but some were. And each child that identified as gay was another relationship severed between Christian parents and their child. Not only that, once the LGBT lifestyle became accepted, the churches were forced to hire LGBT preachers or shut down. Some even did it willingly in an attempt to appeal to a younger audience. Once a gay pastor was in the pulpit, the church could be assumed fallen.

"The police continued to leave and, as a result, the rioters were able to destroy the larger cities. Christianity was attacked as evil and full of hate. Any men willing to speak out against this machine were silenced. The cities brought in federal troops to control the riots, or so we were told. We later learned the troops brought in had been specifically questioned and chosen for loyalty to the leaders of the cities they were assigned. Then came the Coup.

"This is what you know of as the Ascension. One day, all of our communications to the cities were cut off. That same day, another country named China attacked. It took a while for many of us to learn because our media was silent on it, but they attacked the rural areas first. We aren't sure but we think they were planning on controlling our food. America is a very resource rich land with some of the most productive farm land in the world. Control of that land could lead to control of the world.

"Large helicopters full of troops descended in various places throughout the country. The elites had an agreement with the Chinese troops to allow them to land. They even did part of it through the legal system. A few elites had bought most of the farmland and sold it all at once to the Chinese government. At the same time China invaded, the elites took control of the cities. Federal troops stationed inside cities became guards over the inhabitants. Any not loyal to the leaders were killed and the leaders demanded worship of all those living.

"No one expected the rural people to fight back. But we fought. And we fought *hard*. While the cities were isolating and cowering, the rural areas had been preparing. Guns and ammo had been sold out all over the country for months while people were stocking up. The rural people were ready. That first invasion attempt was quashed almost immediately as small towns gathered together and fought back.

"Once it was finished, the remnants of the federal government got together and figured out what had happened. Our internet was repaired and communications were re-established. We were able to view the online history of the leaders of our old government. Those in power, the elite, had lied and cheated to get positions in government. They had been doing it for years, but once they got control of the voting machines, the people's only chance at control was taken away.

"Once the elite had enough power and control, they began a plan with China to sell out America while they retained control of the larger cities. The federal army members stationed in the cities were able to quickly and easily implement marshal law. Each city became in island unto itself as they were divided up by the wealthy elite.

"The elites became dictators in their own lands, controlling the people with their own personal armies. Each city had a population of people able and willing to do the work needed to function. The cities all had their own method of population management, but slavery was very common. Christianity was universally denounced as the elites began calling themselves 'gods.'

"While the cities have floundered, the rural areas have flourished. A new government has been established without the presence of the cities. A government you will be offered to take part in. If you qualify, you will be an equal partner in our government. A partner with rights and responsibilities.

"These will be explained to you over the course of the next few months as you continue through the classes. If you choose to join us, you will be given a place to live and a stipend for three months while you are given instruction on a skill of your choice. This skill will allow you to find a job in a community that you join. After the three month education period, you will be expected to provide for yourself. No further assistance is provided by the government, though there are local programs that do offer assistance if needed.

"We are taking you now to the closest education camp. However, you are not forced to join us. If what I've told you doesn't seem real or you don't feel capable of providing for yourself, we will bring you to a separate city where you can continue to live as you have been living. Just know that if you decide to do that, we may not be able to come in to get you. We are working to reclaim as many of the cities as we can, but it is difficult to muster support for places that betrayed us."

Zack put down his booklet and looked at them. He sighed and said, "OK, I think that's all. That's my whole presentation. What do you think?" He sat quietly and looked at them. Rhys wasn't sure what to say. He looked to the equally astounded face of his wife.

"Uh," Rhys began. "I guess I'm not really sure what to say."

"Well, first thing and I'm pretty sure I know the answer but I just want to be clear," Zack replied. "Do you want to join our community?"

Rhys felt his mouth break into a huge smile. "Yes, of course."

Zack smiled and said, "Yeah I figured. And you guys, too right?" He looked over Rhys's shoulder to his children.

"Yes," their voices rang out from the back seat. They sounded genuinely excited about the idea.

"OK, well that settles that then. Do you guys have any questions?"

"Does anyone actually say no?" Rhys replied.

"You'd be surprised," Zack said. His shoulders dropped a little. "We've gotten more out from other cities, but I'd guess it's almost a quarter that decide they want to stay but be taken to a different city.

That's one of the main reasons we haven't reclaimed some of these cities, actually. We still have people that think living there would be better or easier than making their own living. There are even some from our own populace that willingly decide to move to those cities instead of working to take care of themselves. I'm sure you've seen a few of them in your city.

"They know what it's like in there, right?" Rhys said.

"Some do, but most don't believe it can't really be that bad," Zack said. "I do have to say, from what we've heard, yours is about as bad as it gets. My group has been trying for a while to convince enough people to help to take that city back once and for all. We've had mixed results so far."

"Wouldn't the government do it?" Rhys asked.

"They'd help," Zack replied, "but they wouldn't do it without the local support. I've been keeping my eye out, hoping to help someone like you. Someone from the inside escape. You can give a first-hand account of what life is actually like in there. That will go a long way to convincing people."

Rhys sat quietly for a minute, looking out the window. Then a small voice spoke out from the back seat. "What about Charles?" Lily asked. Rhys looked back at Lily and smiled. He saw her eyes filled with tears, but she gave him a brave smile back. "Yeah, people would fight for Charles. If they knew what happened."

"What happened?" Zack asked. Rhys quickly told him the story of Charles's death and crucifixion. Zack looked stunned. He seemed lost for words for a moment as he stared at Rhys. "That actually happened?" he finally said.

"I saw it with my own eyes," Rhys replied. "Actually, I helped build the cross myself, though that was only so I wouldn't stand out in the crowd when I refused the stone Charles's parents."

"WHAT?! A stoning? Like from Bible times stoning?" Zack looked horrified.

"Yeah," Rhys said. He was a little confused about the man's strong response. "I thought you said you knew what went on in there."

"Well," Zack said gaining some composure. He pulled out a small black box, long and flat. He separated two parts and sat it on his lap. The top screen filled with light.

"What's that," Rhys asked.

"Oh, my laptop," Zack replied over his shoulder. He was tapping something on the bottom and looking at the light. "It's the internet so I can talk to people. When did this happen?" Zack's voice had turned very serious. He was intently focused on something new.

"Uh," Rhys replied, "it was the day after we tried to escape last week. The morning after. Just after morning bell."

"OK, thanks," Zack replied. He kept punching some things onto the box. After a few minutes, Zack sat back, putting his hands together and looking up. Rhys smiled at the realization the man was praying. Openly and publicly he was praying. Rhys felt a shiver run down his spine.

Once he finished praying, Zack turned and moved the screen back so they could see it. On the screen was a picture of a street full of people. It was taken from almost straight above, but Rhys could make out himself and his wife. The picture was moving and he realized he was watching a memory.

"It's a video recording," Zack explained. "This is a series of pictures showing exactly what happened that day." Rhys watched as the scene played out ending with Charles on the cross. Rhys felt a wave of nausea filling his stomach at the memory.

"Yeah that was the day," Rhys said. "Why did you show us that?"

Zack looked at them and his face fell a little. "Oh, sorry. I shouldn't have done that. That was very tactless of me, I'm sorry. I just was so excited I wanted to see for myself, but I didn't think how it would affect you."

Rhys nodded appreciation and put his arm around his wife who was crying into her arm. "Thanks. Why are you so excited about it?"

Zack swallowed and took a deep breath. "You're daughter is right. This'll do it. This is exactly what we need if we are going to show people how terrible things truly are in there. Video proof of what you've been through. What people are still going through living in this city. We have been trying to get pictures of the abuse and torture we know is happening in there, but haven't had any luck. The leaders of your city are smart and they always do this stuff indoors or under cover. We've even had people flown in to examine things, but they haven't seen any abuses either.

"This is a great thing. With this video, I guarantee my group will be able to get full support to reclaim the city. Those in charge will be captured and jailed and the Colors will be given the same explanation you were given. They will have to make their choice but at least they will have a choice. And those in power won't be able to hurt anyone like they did your friends.

"Thank God for you and your family. Thank God for your bravery and courage. We can save that city."

Rhys smiled and looked to his wife and his children in the back. He gave his wife a kiss and settled in for the ride. They continued talking for the rest of the trip, Rhys growing more excited by the minute. When they finally arrived at their destination a few hours later the van stopped.

Zack turned in his seat and said, "It has truly been an honor to help you. You are going to be a great blessing to whatever city you end up in. Before you go start your new life, I would like to offer you a blessing if that is OK?" Rhys nodded his assent and bowed his head. Zack said:

"May the Lord bless you and keep you.

"May the Lord cause His face to shine upon you, and be gracious to you.

"May the Lord lift up His countenance upon you, and give you peace.

"Amen."

ABOUT THE AUTHOR

Matt Nath is a young, Christian man trying to follow God while balancing being a father, husband, and Funeral Director. He never thought he'd be able to add author to that list, but through the help and grace of God, it happened!

Matt lives in a small town in Minnesota with his wife and three children. He lives on mission as a husband and father first, but also finds great fulfillment through his full-time career as a Funeral Director working as a part of a team at a local, family-owned funeral home. He is also involved with his local church, helping to lead the youth group, participating in men's groups, and spreading the love of Jesus to those in his community.

When he isn't with his family or working, Matt enjoys playing complex, deeply strategic board games, both with a local group and alone. Matt is also an avid reader and creative writer. An entire wall of his house is filled with books and board games, almost all of which show signs of wear. Matt is almost always found with his wife of over ten years, Tracie. They work together raising their children, fixing up their house, gardening, thrift shopping, antiquing, and traveling. Keeping the kids busy and out of trouble is a full-time job in itself, but Matt and Tracie work hard to keep their children in the light of God and help them understand their place and God's purpose for them in our fallen world.

CPSIA information can be obtained
at www.ICGtesting.com
Printed in the USA
BVHW070559160122
625952BV00001B/44